THE HAUNTING AT CLIFF HOUSE

Karleen Bradford

Cover by Laurie McGaw

Scholastic-TAB Publications Ltd.
123 Newkirk Road, Richmond Hill, Ontario
Canada

Canadian Cataloguing in Publication Data

Bradford, Karleen
    The haunting at Cliff House

ISBN 0-590-71517-8

I. Title

PS8553.R32H38 1985   jC813'.54   C85-098475-0
PZ7.B72Ha 1985

12 11 10 9 8 7 6 5 4 3 2 1   9   6 7 8 9/8 0 1/9

for Carolyn

Contents

Pronunciation Guide

Aberidris	Ah-ber-*id*-riss
Aberystwyth	Ah-ber-*ust*-with (*th* as in *thin*)
Bronwen	*Bron*-wen
Catrin	*Kah*-trin
Gareth	*Gah*-reth (*th* as in *thin*)
Llanafron	*Chlah*-nah-vron (*ch* as in *loch*)
Meiriona	My-ree-*oh*-nuh
Morfudd	*More*-vuth (*th* as in *then*)
Noddwr	*Nah*-ther (*th* as in *then*)
Pen-y-Craig	Pen-ee-*craig*

1

The house on the cliff

The big stone house stood, grim and forbidding, almost at the very edge of the cliff. Far below, the ocean crashed and snarled in huge, breaking waves against the rocks. The walls of the house were made of thick, drab grey blocks of stone, and the slate roof shone blackly in the rain. Alison shivered. This lonely, wild place was not what she had imagined when her father had told her they were going to spend the summer in Wales.

"We're off to Wales!" he had announced in glee two weeks before. "Just for the summer. But it should give me time to get a good start on that novel that's been running around inside my head. No friends or colleagues to distract me. Getting this house is a gift from the gods — although I'm sorry poor old Great-aunt What's-her-name died, of course, bless her soul," he added hastily.

Her father's ties with Wales had long been cut and the news that he had inherited a house from a distantly related, never even heard of, great-aunt had come as a surprise.

"We'll leave as soon as school's out," he had announced enthusiastically.

This had not given them much time to organize, but Alison's father had never been one to worry about something like that. Somehow or other he had gotten their passports, arranged for someone to take over his summer classes at the university, and had them both ready to go the day after Alison finished grade eight. He had even managed to sneak in a few crash classes in Welsh.

Alison sighed and pushed back the tangled, sandy curls that always seemed to be in her eyes. She had not had too much to say about the whole affair. As far as she could remember, her father hadn't even thought to ask her if she wanted to go. She was used to that, though. Truth to tell, she rather enjoyed it. Ever since her mother had died when Alison was very small, she and her father had had a close relationship. Living with him was unsettling — but different. Her grandmother had halfheartedly offered to take her in for the summer, but she preferred to go with him.

Still, she had expected something a little more civilized than this. Great-aunt What's-her-name must have been a real recluse!

Her father didn't seem at all taken aback, however. He stood beside Alison, staring up at the house in delight. "Isn't this something?" he exclaimed.

"It's certainly *something*, all right," she answered.

A slight cough from the taxi driver, who had

finished unloading their bags, startled them. They had forgotten all about him. Mr. Evans paid him, then hoisted up two of the bags and a parcel of groceries they had picked up on the way. "Well," he said, "let's see what it's like inside."

Alison reached for her suitcase and her overnight bag. She followed him up the path to the front door through a garden that was really not much more than a tangle of weeds and wild, runaway bushes.

"That'll give me something to do when the typewriter gets too much for me," Mr. Evans said, looking around him. Gardening was another of his passions and Alison knew he would regard these grounds as a challenge.

A high stone wall ran out towards the back from either side of the house, ending almost at the cliff's edge. Through an old gate standing half open Alison could see that the back garden looked just as untamed. "Lots of luck," she said dryly. "Just don't ask me to help." Gardening was not a passion she shared with her father.

"Oh, don't worry. You'll probably have lots to do inside. Remember, you volunteered to cook this summer."

"Volunteered! *Was* volunteered, you mean," Alison answered indignantly.

"Nonsense. I distinctly heard you say 'I'll take over the cooking this summer, Daddy dear, so you'll be free to write the novel that's going to make us rich.'"

Alison laughed. "You'll be sorry," she warned

3

ominously. She started to say something else but stopped. A stone carving over the front door had suddenly caught her eye. It was a dragon, painted bright red, rearing up on its hind legs with its front claws outstretched. From its back grew enormous wings, and its tongue licked out fiercely. Underneath it were carved the words, *Pen-y-Craig*. Something seemed very forbidding about it to Alison.

"Dad, look."

Mr. Evans looked at her, puzzled by the sudden note of urgency in her voice. Then he looked up at the dragon. "What's the matter, Alison? It's just a dragon. The dragon's the symbol of Wales, you know. Just as the rose is the symbol of England. I expect we'll see dragons carved all over the place here."

Even to herself, Alison couldn't explain the uneasy feeling that had taken possession of her. "Those words," she asked hesitantly, "what do they mean?"

"Pen-y-Craig," Mr. Evans read. He dropped the suitcases he was holding and reached into his pocket. Pulling out a pocket dictionary, he leafed through it, muttering. "*Pen* means top, I know that . . . Ah, yes. Rock. Top of the rock — top of the cliff. That's what it means."

"It's certainly that," Alison whispered. The roar of the ocean below drowned out her words.

Mr. Evans unlocked the door and held it open for her. She shook off the strange feeling and stepped through into a long hall.

On either side of them were large rooms with great, heavy oak beams stretching across the ceilings. One room had a long table with chairs around it, the other seemed to be a living room or parlour. Both were crammed full of furniture, clocks, bric-a-brac and dark, looming pictures. At the far end of the hall was the kitchen. Alison could see an ancient stove leaning dejectedly against the wall. She certainly would have her work cut out for her if she was going to have to cook on that. A staircase with a tattered, musty-looking carpet on it ran up from the hall and disappeared into the murkiness above.

The house was clean, the estate people had seen to that, but the smell of the sea had seeped into the shut-up rooms and hung rankly and damply in the air.

"What an incredible place," Mr. Evans said. "It looks like a museum!"

"Like a haunted museum," Alison said, then wished she hadn't. Her voice echoed in the empty hall and seemed to die there.

"Come on. Let's explore." Her father was off and up the stairs, two at a time.

She followed him reluctantly. At the top she paused. She was in a dark, panelled hall with rooms off both sides. She could hear her father banging around in one of them, calling her to come and look at the view, but she stayed where she was.

There was something wrong. Something *felt* wrong.

Alison stood, her head tilted to one side as if

listening. Had she heard a voice calling her name? Impossible. And yet . . . She wished her father would be quiet for a moment.

There. Again! A shiver ran down her spine and suddenly she felt cold. She looked at the closed door of the room in front of her. At that moment she felt sure someone was in there. Calling her.

Her father burst out of the room down at the end. "There's a desk in there — would you believe it? A huge old desk! They must have known a writer was coming to live here." Then he bounded past her back towards the stairs. "I'm going to go down and see if I can get a fire going somewhere," he announced. "Take the chill off a bit. It's cold — even if it is supposed to be summer."

Alison paid hardly any attention to him. She was staring at the door, almost as if she expected it to open by itself. Not really wanting to, but unable to stop herself, she crossed the hall and put her hand on the knob. She stood for another moment, listening again. Nothing.

Slowly she turned the knob and pushed the door open.

The room was big, with a window on the far side looking out over the ocean. It was almost dark now, and the corners were filled with shadows. Alison stepped in. The door swung shut behind her and she jumped, startled, as it slammed. For a moment she almost panicked, but she caught herself.

It's the uneven floors, she thought. They're tilty. Old houses are often tilty. Doors swing open and shut all the time.

The room was unnaturally quiet. Alison realized that for the first time since they'd got out of the taxi she couldn't hear the noise of the sea. She walked over to the window and looked out, as if to reassure herself that it was still there. Of course it was. In the darkening evening she could see the white caps of the waves as they dashed towards the cliff on which the house sat. A few seagulls and kittiwakes were still wheeling and circling far out above the angry water. Rain had begun to spatter at the windowpane, and suddenly the wind came up. An unexpected blast shook the glass violently, shattering the silence. As if sound everywhere had been turned on again, the roar of the waves, too, invaded the room.

Just then Alison had the distinct impression that someone was watching her. She turned around quickly, expecting to see her father, but there was no one there. "Dad?" The word faded away as if it had never been spoken.

The room was still empty.

She looked around at the shadows. For the first time she realized that all the furniture was shrouded in white dust covers. Indistinct shapes gleamed faintly in the dusk.

The feeling that something was wrong came over her again, even more strongly than before. And something else as well.

It feels as if it's waiting, she thought. As if this whole room is gathered around me, waiting. And then, out of the darkness, she heard a voice.

Alison!

Her name echoed in the room. It hadn't been

spoken aloud. She was certain of that. But she had heard it. She had!

Alison ran for the door and out into the hall. Slamming it herself this time, she darted across the hall and leaned against the wall, gasping, staring at the closed door. Someone was in there. Someone who knew her name! Even as she thought it, she heard the voice again, whispering in her mind.

Alison. You must come back, Alison. You must!

2
A ghost?

Alison dashed down the stairs. There were banging noises and muffled curses coming from the kitchen. She headed towards them, then suddenly checked herself. What was she going to say? "We have to get out of here, Dad — the house is haunted"?

Knowing her father, he would either laugh at her or ask for details so he could put them in his book.

Besides, she told herself sternly, I *must* have imagined it. Not enough sleep. The trip over on the airplane. The long drive from the airport. Of course she had imagined it. Down here, away from that room, everything seemed totally normal and she was beginning to feel silly.

A sudden crash, followed by more not-so-muffled curses, decided her. She took a deep breath and went into the kitchen.

It was a large room that stretched along the whole length of the house at the back. The slate floor was scrubbed and shining and the big stone fireplace at one end looked as if it might be in good working order. There was a door that must lead out to the back garden. Mr. Evans was struggling through it with an oversized armful of wood. One piece had already dropped; several more seemed about to.

"Here," Alison called, "let me help you, Dad."

The rain was beating in through the open door and her father was soaking wet. He kicked the door shut as Alison unloaded some of the wood from his arms.

"Whew! Thanks."

Together they made the fire, then set about unpacking the groceries and getting a meal ready. True to their private tradition for special occasions, they had splurged on steak and fresh asparagus, and Mr. Evans had treated himself to a small bottle of wine. Alison dug around in the huge old cupboards and came up with an enormous cast-iron frying pan and a somewhat dilapidated pot. A further search uncovered a surprisingly fresh and pretty flowered cotton tablecloth. She covered the unpainted wooden table that stood in the middle of the room and drew up two ladder-backed chairs.

"An antique dealer in Ottawa would kill for these," she remarked, looking at them appraisingly. She loved old things, as did her father, and their apartment back home was furnished with a small but good collection of antiques.

In a very short time they were sitting down to their first dinner in Wales. The fire burned brightly. They had turned out all the lights and lit a small stub of a candle Alison had found and placed

10

in the centre of the table. She had propped it up in a jam jar for want of a better candle holder. The whole effect was warm and cosy, heightened by the sound of the rain drumming on the roof and against the windows.

Mr. Evans raised his glass of wine. "Here's to Wales," he said.

"And a super summer," Alison responded, raising her glass of milk. She looked around her and sighed with contentment, sniffing the delicious smell of steak. Surely nothing could go wrong here. They *were* going to have a great summer, she knew it. She thought briefly of the room upstairs, then pushed it out of her mind, thankful that she hadn't said anything to her father about it. Obviously what she had heard in there was just the result of an overactive and tired mind. Tomorrow in the clear, cold light of day, she'd go back and explore it more thoroughly and laugh at herself for being scared of shadows.

The next morning she was awakened by sunlight streaming through her window and the smell of bacon frying. Throwing on jeans and a shirt, she tore out of her room and down the stairs. Her father was singing lustily as he poked at a sizzling, spitting frying pan.

"I'll do that," Alison said, grabbing for the fork he was holding and turning down the gas under the pan. "It's too hot, Dad — you'll cremate it. And besides, you don't need to fry bacon in butter!"

"And good morning to you too, Alison," Mr. Evans boomed good-naturedly, surrendering the fork. "What shall we do after breakfast? Explore the beach or go into the village for supplies?"

"Village for supplies," Alison answered practically. "Let's save the beach for this afternoon when we're all settled."

"Okay. Eat up, then, and let's get going. It's a grand day! Couldn't be better."

His enthusiasm was catching. Alison found herself humming happily as she drained the bacon and started toast. There didn't seem to be a toaster, so she just held the bread over the gas flame on a fork. It came out a little black in spots, but it tasted good anyway when they slathered it with the fresh country butter they'd bought the day before.

The nearest town of any size was Aberidris, a few kilometres up the coast, but the village of Llanarfon was just a short walk away. As soon as they had finished breakfast, Alison and her father started out. The road was really little more than a narrow track, and the hedgerows, studded with tiny purple, yellow and white wildflowers, reached high above their heads on either side. It was almost as if they were walking in a tunnel. Here and there were rickety wooden fences through which they could see sheep grazing peacefully in the fields beyond.

Soon they came to a white stone cottage with a neat garden in front. An elderly lady was sitting in a rocking chair, dozing in the sun on the tiny front porch. As they passed, she looked up. She seemed to be very old indeed.

"Good morning," Mr. Evans called out loudly.

The old lady just sat staring at them. Alison looked back over her shoulder as they passed. The woman had turned her head to look after them, and there was a strange expression on her face. It struck Alison as one of fear.

That's silly, she told herself. Then, all of a sudden, the sun seemed to dim. Once again Alison was filled with uneasiness, the way she had been when she had first seen the dragon and the words *Pen-y-Craig* carved above it. But this time it was much stronger. She shuddered and rubbed at her bare arms. Goosebumps had popped out in spite of the heat.

Her father looked down. "What's the matter?" he asked.

"That old lady — " Alison stopped. How could she explain? Suddenly she thought of the room in the house. She hadn't gone back into it yet — she hadn't had time. But why should the look on the old lady's face remind her of that?

"She probably didn't hear me," her father said cheerfully. "She's so old, she's probably quite deaf." Nothing seemed to be bothering him.

By noon they had finished their shopping and made the acquaintance of Mrs. Jones-the-Bakery, Mr. Hughes-the-Ironmongery, Mr. Williams-the-Barbershop, Mrs. Humphreys-the-Greengrocery and Mr. Gethin-the-Shop. The whole village had heard that foreigners from Canada were going to spend the summer in the old Evans house — Cliff House, as everyone around there seemed to call it — and everyone on the High Street had come out to

meet them. Mr. Evans had basked in their friend-
liness and Alison had received at least a dozen
invitations to come and meet the well-wishers'
children. There would be no lack of company this
summer if she wanted it, that was certain. Alison
wasn't too sure that she did, though. She'd always
been shy with strangers, quite the opposite of her
father. She was prepared for a quiet, solitary summer of reading and exploring on her own. Her
father was company enough for her.

As they headed back towards home, Mr.
Evans suddenly stopped. "Would you look at
that?" he said. "A library! Who would have imagined a village this size would have a library? Come
on, Alison, let's have a look."

Mr. Evans was a library addict and Alison
knew there would be no getting him away until he
had investigated this one. With a sigh of re-
signation, she followed him in. It was getting quite
hot now and she would much rather have hurried
back to explore the beach.

And that room, a voice inside her insisted.
First you have to explore that room. Just to prove
to yourself there's really nothing there. Or nobody.

The library was very small. A dark-haired
woman was seated at a desk just inside the entrance. Through a narrow doorway Alison could
see a boy of about fifteen stacking books on
shelves. They were the only two people there. As
Alison and her father came in, the woman smiled
and stood up. She was younger than Alison had at
first thought.

"I'm Richard Evans," Alison's father said, striding forward with his hand outstretched. "And this is my daughter, Alison. We're — "

"You're the 'foreigners' from Canada," the woman said with a laugh, "come to stay with us this summer. I know. There's been talk of nothing else around here for weeks. Welcome to Llanarfon. I'm Meiriona Ellis."

Her voice was low and vibrant, with the same lilt to it that Alison had heard in the voices of the other Welsh people they had met. As the woman smiled at her, Alison realized with a start that she was beautiful. Meiriona turned to speak to Mr. Evans again and he looked almost dazed.

For some reason she couldn't understand, Alison felt a sudden resentment towards the lovely woman standing in front of them. For the rest of the time her father talked to Meiriona, Alison stared resolutely at the books on the shelves around her, hardly answering when she was spoken to. Even when Meiriona called the boy in the other room to come and meet them, she barely raised her eyes to look at him.

"This is my brother Gareth. He goes to school in Aberidris during the year, but comes home to help me in the summer." The boy was also dark-haired and looked very like his sister.

Alison muttered an indistinct acknowledgement of the introduction and went back to studying the books. Her father didn't seem to notice anything unusual about her behaviour, however, and this increased her resentment.

"Imagine meeting a woman like that in Llanarfon," Mr. Evans exclaimed as they left the library and once again headed back to the house. "I wonder what in the world she's doing buried here! She's obviously extremely well educated. Too much so to be mouldering away in this place, I should say."

"Just an old maid with nothing better to do, I guess," Alison said acidly.

Her father looked at her, amazed. "Old maid? You — my liberated-to-the-nth-degree daughter who only last month announced that she didn't think she'd ever bother with marriage — *you* are talking about *old maids*?"

Alison flushed and didn't answer.

As soon as they reached the house Alison ran up the stairs, intending to go to her room. But the closed door across the hall held her suddenly immobile. Almost in a trance, she found herself moving towards it. She opened it and stepped into the room, willing it to look ordinary, ordering herself not to be frightened, her heart to stop pounding.

Once again she was closed off in absolute silence.

Today sunlight streamed in through the window. Dust motes danced in the watery beams striking across the room onto the cloths covering the furniture. For some reason the estate people hadn't tidied up this room. Alison's eyes were drawn to an enormous fireplace along one wall. It was so big a person could step right inside it. As if she were sleepwalking, she crossed over to it and knelt down. The feeling that someone was watching her came over her again, as it had the night before. This time she couldn't pull herself away.

Images crowded into Alison's mind. She closed her eyes and gradually they took shape. She recognized the room she was now in, although it was much brighter and cleaner. A fire lit up the fireplace, and several pieces of dark, polished furniture gleamed in the reflected light. A canopied bed stood along the opposite wall, with a rag doll lying propped up against the pillows. A dim, wavery figure was sitting on a three-legged stool in front of the fire. It seemed to be a girl. She was writing something in a small brown book on her knee.

Alison squeezed her eyes tightly shut in an effort to make the figure come clear, but instead everything became more blurry. She could tell only that the girl was about her own age and that she was dressed in odd, old-fashioned clothes. Her hair, long and dark, fell around her shoulders.

The girl rose. She picked at one of the bricks on the far side of the fireplace, then pulled it right out of the wall. Quickly she put her book into the hole and pushed the brick back. Alison strained to see more, but the scene grew dark and finally disappeared. She opened her eyes and there was the room as it had been — dust-covered and silent.

What is happening to me? she thought. She stared at the fireplace. The bricks looked absolutely solid, as if they hadn't been disturbed since they'd been laid. Still, she couldn't resist reaching out and running her hand down over them, feeling their rough edges scratch against her palm. What nonsense! And yet . . . which one had it been? Was it this one? No. It had been lower down. This one? Yes! She was sure of it. It was right on the edge of the fireplace and it had been chipped on a corner, just as this one was. She curled her fingers around the edges of it and pulled. Nothing happened.

I knew it wouldn't, she told herself, but then she tugged at it again. It still didn't budge. Alison looked around for something sharp and saw an old brass letter opener lying on the floor under one of the covered pieces of furniture. She picked it up and began to pry at the brick in earnest. Suddenly it came loose. She took it in both hands and gently worked it out. There was a space behind it — and in the space was a small brown book.

3

The hidden diary

For a moment Alison just stared at the book, then she reached in and pulled it out. Immediately all the fear she had felt before rushed back, almost overwhelming her again. She turned around quickly and pressed her back against the fireplace. Her eyes darted nervously around the room, but everything remained the same.

Finally, hardly daring to breathe, she looked down at the book in her hands. She ran her fingers hesitantly over the smooth, hard cover. Then, taking a deep breath, she opened it.

The book was so old and brittle that a piece of the cover broke off as she turned it. It would have to be handled very carefully. On the first page she could just make out some faint, spidery writing. It was hard to understand, but at least it was in English, not Welsh.

Alison wondered about that as she stared at it, trying to make out the words. Then she remembered her father had told her that even long ago many of the Welsh had been educated in English as well as their own language. There was a date across the top, then the writing began.

With her heart thumping so loudly she could hear it in her ears, Alison began to read:

The fourteenth day of April in the year 1810.

My name is Bronwen. Last week I celebrated my thirteenth birthday. It was probably the last pleasant birthday I shall ever know. Yesterday my father brought me here to Pen-y-Craig to live and I hated the house on sight. It is a terrible, lonely place. To think that I am to be forced to live here from now on is unbearable. I can't be happy here. I won't! Somehow I must get away. How could anyone ever imagine that my father, who was one of the wealthiest and most respected of all the ships' captains in Aberystwyth, would ever want to build himself such an ugly, horrible house away out here on the top of a cliff? It's so lonely. So far away from everything I've ever known and loved. And the wind never stops blowing!

Alison looked up at the window, where the wind was rattling the panes as usual. Then, irresistibly, her eyes were drawn back to the diary.

It's not as if he were an old man. He's much too young to retire and bury himself up here. It's just because he misses my mother so much — I'm sure it is. Nothing has been the same since she died! He would never have brought her here, I know it. I'm sure I shall die of loneliness. He says I'll like it better when Catrin arrives to be my governess and companion, but I won't. She's just a distant cousin of ours who never got married, and I'm sure I'll not have anything in common with her . . .

The door flew open as if rocked by an explosion, and Mr. Evans barged in. He had his bathing suit on and a towel wound around his neck.

"Here you are. I've been looking all over the house for you. Didn't you hear me calling you? I thought you wanted to explore the beach!"

With one quick movement Alison kicked the book out of sight behind her. She was shaking with the shock, and her knees felt as if they might give way at any second.

"For heaven's sake, Dad. Couldn't you have knocked?" Her voice was shrill.

Mr. Evans stared at her in amazement. "But this isn't even your room," he sputtered.

Alison collected herself with an effort. "I'm sorry," she said quickly. "It's just that you scared me. It must be this room. There's something about it . . ." The words trailed off as she looked around her. With her father here, and the sun pouring in, the room looked normal enough.

Her father gave her a quizzical look, then shrugged. "It is funny, isn't it," he said. "It's the only room in the house that wasn't tidied up for us. Maybe you could do that later on. In the meantime, let's at least open the window — it's terribly hot and stuffy in here."

He walked over to the window and pulled it

wide open. Immediately the moist, fishy smell of the sea rushed in, and Alison could hear the wild, despairing cries of the seabirds as they swooped and dove at the waves. Always, just as they seemed about to plunge into the water, they pulled up and back into the sky.

"Well, are you coming?" Mr. Evans was obviously eager to get going.

Alison hesitated. "In — in a minute. You go ahead. I'll just change and be right down."

As soon as her father left the room she retrieved the book and stuffed it back into the hole. Her hands were shaking as she fitted the brick back into place.

All the time she was changing, her mind was whirling. First there had been the sinister dragon over the door, then the voice calling her name. Then — what had it been? A vision? Now this frightening coincidence. The girl in the diary was the same age as she was. And Bronwen had arrived at Pen-y-Craig with her father just as she, Alison had. Could it have been Bronwen who had called out? But how? The date on the diary was 1810! Bronwen would have grown up, been an old woman, would be *dead* by now!

"Alison! Hurry up!"

She grabbed a towel and ran down the stairs to her waiting father.

There didn't seem to be any way down the cliffs behind their house, so they walked along the road until it joined a path that led up from the beach. It was only a short distance from there to the water. The beach was pebbly and full of stones up above the high-level mark, but as far as the water reached, it was smooth, hard-packed sand. The wind was brisk, but the sun was warm. In spite of all that had happened, Alison found herself looking forward to a swim. When the tide had gone out, it had left dozens of little pools in the sand behind it. She bent down to look at a tiny pink crab in one of them. It looked so fragile. She wondered how it felt when the great waves of water rushed over it and buried it beneath them.

The tide was coming back in now, and she and her father walked out to meet it. The first wave hit their ankles and ran swirling back out around their feet. Alison gasped. The icy coldness of the water was a shock. Suddenly the idea of a swim was much less appealing. Her father flinched too, but recovered quickly.

"Come on, chicken," he called. "You're not afraid of a little cold water, are you?" He started to trot, then threw himself into the waves.

Alison gritted her teeth and launched herself after him.

The water was too cold to stand for long, however, and after a few minutes they had both had enough. They raced each other back out, towelled themselves dry and warmed up again in the hot sun.

"I think I'll go back up to the house and get organized," Mr. Evans said finally. "I did come here to work and the sooner I get started the better, I guess. Are you coming up?"

Alison looked around. The beach stretched invitingly along the coast. Then she thought of Bronwen's diary waiting for her to come back, hidden behind the brick. For a moment she wavered, undecided. But it was so peaceful here. Suddenly she had no desire whatsoever to go back up to that gloomy old house — back up to Bronwen's problems.

"I think I'll explore around here for a while," she said.

"Okay," her father answered. "See you later."

Back along the cliff, near their house, was a point of rocks stretching out towards the water. Beyond that, right underneath the house, there seemed to be a cove. It looked inviting and Alison decided to explore it. She walked around the point, noticing idly that the tide had come in quite a bit just in the short time they'd been down there.

Once inside the cove, Alison felt as if she were cut off from the whole world. There was another point of rocks on the other side, so that the beach was completely isolated. This is where I'll come when I want to be alone, she thought delightedly. This can be my own private spot.

She was directly underneath the house now and couldn't see it anymore. The slope was steep and covered with bracken and low bushes. It looked unclimbable. Then she saw two huge black rocks right at the bottom of the cliff. There was a dark opening gaping between them, and in the hot, shiny-hard sunshine it looked deep and mysterious. Curious, she walked over to it. It was a cave, and as she approached it she realized that it was much bigger than she had thought. The air coming out of it was cool and dank.

To Alison it looked gloomy and uninviting, but the sun beating down on her was very hot by now, and the dried salt-sea water on her body made her itchy. She stood for a moment weighing the advantages of getting in out of the sun against a strong, almost unreasonable reluctance to step into the shadows of that cave.

You are a coward lately, Alison Evans, she told herself in exasperation. You seem to be afraid of everything! Taking a deep breath, she walked into the damp darkness. But almost immediately, she wished she hadn't. The feeling of something wrong that she had felt in Bronwen's room was present even more strongly here. Alison took a half-step backwards, then forced herself to look around her. The walls, even the ceiling, were dripping with water.

The sea must come in and fill this whole cave up at high tide, she thought uneasily.

Ahead of her she could see the dim outlines of what looked like a ledge. She barely glanced at it before turning to go back out. She felt she couldn't stand another moment inside. Just then she heard a noise. Above the faraway roar of the sea there was a scrabbling, scratching sound.

Alison froze. The noise was coming from the ledge. She looked back towards it, tensing herself to run. Something had shifted there in the shadows! For a moment she couldn't move, and in that second she heard another sound: a meow.

A cat! Almost laughing with relief, she ran forward and peered up over the edge of the ledge. There, backed as far away from her as it could get, sat a wild-looking cat, hunched against the dripping rock wall. When it saw her coming closer it hissed fiercely.

What in the world do I do now? Alison thought in exasperation. I can't possibly go back out and leave that cat in here. When the tide comes in it'll drown!

Slowly, cautiously, she pulled herself up onto the ledge. The cat hissed again. Alison sat down as close to it as she dared and began talking in a low, soothing voice. Gradually the cat seemed to calm down and accept her presence. Alison looked around. How was she ever going to get it out? It didn't look very friendly. She put out a hand to pat it; the cat lashed out viciously and scratched her, then glared at her with baleful eyes.

"I should just leave you here to your fate," she muttered. "What a bad-tempered, ungrateful animal you are!" She half rose to go, then sank back. She couldn't just leave it.

She sat talking to it, trying to get it used to her, then put her hand out again. This time the cat yowled indignantly and leaped off the ledge. Before Alison realized what was happening, it had raced out through the mouth of the cave.

"Great!" she muttered again, feeling like a fool. "Here I've just wasted half an hour in this disgusting cave, trying to rescue a bad-tempered cat that didn't need rescuing at all. It probably comes in here every day for a nap!" And she turned around on her knees to back off the ledge.

She jumped to the ground and looked towards the opening. She'd come farther in than she had realized. The cat, of course, was gone. All Alison could see were her own footprints in the wet sand and the faint imprint of the cat's paws. Soon she became aware of something else — a strange, rhythmic, booming sound. She stood for a moment, trying to figure out what it was, then realized it was the sound of the waves. But now it was much closer, much louder.

The tide! Could it have come in that quickly?

Alison ran for the entrance. She stopped in horror as she looked at the point of rocks separating her from the rest of the beach. The sea was already lapping around it, licking at it with tongues of foam. She glanced at the point on the other side of the cove. It was completely under water. She was trapped!

4

Bronwen

Any idea Alison might have had about swimming around the point vanished as soon as she reached it. The waves had completely covered the end and were quickly, greedily engulfing the rest of it. They were crashing and breaking with such force she knew she could never swim through them. She looked up at the rocks above her. She would have to climb over them if she were going to escape. With each wave the water was reaching higher and higher, and even as she stood, irresolute, it rose up to her ankles.

Alison reached up and found a handhold in the rocks. Cautiously she felt for a crack to put her toes into. For a moment she couldn't find any in the smooth rock face and she nearly panicked. Then her toes found a niche. She put her weight on it carefully, drew her other foot up and began feeling for another toehold. Her fingers stretched out, feeling the hard, unyielding rock, searching for handholds. Slowly, bit by bit, she inched upwards. When she was nearly at the top she looked back down and gasped, clutching at the rock face for support. The sea had rushed in below her and was swirling evilly around the rocks, still rising steadily. There was no returning. Alison faced the rock again and reached for another handhold.

Finally her hands were clinging to the top of the point. She slumped for a moment, but the surge of the waves below sent up a shower of spray. There was no time to rest. Panting with the effort, she hauled herself up and over the top. Even then she couldn't stop. The sea was reaching up on the other side too. She had to stagger along the top of the point, slipping and sliding over the loose shale until she was far enough inland to climb down the other side. It was even steeper and higher there.

For a moment Alison fought a feeling of nausea as she peered down at the beach. It seemed so far away. She looked up at the cliff rising away from the point, but there was no escape that way. Climbing up onto the point had been difficult, but scaling that near-vertical cliff would be impossible. The only way was down. She turned around, knelt and began to back over the edge. Not once on the way down did she turn again to look.

At last, incredibly, one searching foot felt sand beneath her. Firm, solid sand. She was on the beach. She had made it! But the tide was still coming in. Exhausted as she was, she forced herself to run up beside the point of rocks until she was well above the high-water mark. Only then did she allow herself to sink down onto the sand and rest.

The first thing that met her eyes, when she

had recovered enough to look around her, was the cat. It was lying on a ledge of rock above her, sunning itself and licking its fur into place. She glared at it.

"You! You're the cause of all this, you know, you wretched creature!"

The cat stopped licking for a moment and looked at her with a condescending, slightly pitying look, then went back to its grooming.

A shout from farther down the beach startled her and she looked up to see someone running towards her. As he drew closer she could see that it was Gareth, the boy she had met in the library. He was wearing a bathing suit and looked as if he had been swimming, but his face was grim.

"Are you all right?" he called as he came closer. "I saw you climbing down off the point. What happened?"

Alison blushed. She might have known. Just to make matters worse!

"I — I was looking around in a cave over there," she started to explain, feeling stupid, "and I found a cat. *That* cat," she added with an annoyed grimace, pointing to the animal that was now busily licking one paw dry and ignoring her completely. "It was up on a ledge in the cave and I thought it was stuck. I tried to get it out, but it ran out by itself. By that time the tide had come in and I was cut off," she finished weakly, feeling more stupid than ever. It sounded so dumb!

Gareth's expression relaxed and he laughed. Alison flushed again.

"That's my cat," the boy explained. "He's a

tough old fellow — you don't have to worry any about him. He likes to come down here with me when I go swimming, and he always naps in that cave because it's so nice and cool in there. He knows exactly when the tide's coming in and he has to get out," he added. "I've watched him. He has it timed almost to the second." He laughed again. "Fancy you trying to rescue *him*!"

Then his face became serious again. "But that cave —" he began. "You shouldn't — " He stopped.

Alison stared at him. For some reason she was almost afraid to hear what he would say next. But he shook his head and forced a smile again. "Oh, it's nothing. It's just — it's just that when I saw you running from it . . ."

"I wasn't running from the cave," Alison interrupted. "I was running from the tide. It was coming in so quickly." Even to herself her words sounded unconvincing and defensive. Had she been running from the cave? Against her will, that feeling she had had of something wrong about the place flooded over her again. But before she could say anything more, Gareth had gone on.

His voice had changed and his words were light and reassuring. Why did Alison feel that he was making a deliberate effort to be casual?

"You must have been frightened," he said. "But you climbed over that point all by yourself. That's quite a climb!"

Alison shook her head to clear away the cobwebs of doubt. "I'd never have been able to do it if I hadn't been so frightened," she admitted.

"Come on. I'll walk you down the beach to your

road," Gareth said. "Have you been for a swim? Do you like the sea? It's cold, isn't it? How do you like Llanarfon, by the way?"

Alison was a little dazed. Which question should she answer first? She looked back once at the point, then resolved to forget the whole experience, cave and all, and not get caught again. Out of the corner of her eye she saw the cat stretch languorously and leap lightly down to follow them. Gareth was talking and pointing at something farther up the beach. She stuck her tongue out at the cat, then turned to see what he was pointing at.

As she did so, a thought slid into a corner of her mind. Gareth had never asked *which* cave she'd been trapped in. Surely there must be others — the cliffs must be honeycombed with them. The cat, of course. He knew which cave his cat napped in. It was a logical explanation, but for some reason it didn't entirely satisfy her. Gareth's next words caught her attention, however, and the thought slid away again as quickly as it had come.

"I was just going over to investigate that when I saw you," he said, apparently not noticing that she hadn't answered him. "I think it's a seal stranded on the beach."

At first all she could see was a black blob, but as they drew closer she saw that it was, indeed, a seal. A round, fat, baby-looking seal.

"Look," Gareth said. "What a mess!"

The seal's fur was all matted and dark with oil, and covered with sand. It had obviously been rolling and rolling on the beach. As they came closer, the animal stared up at them with huge brown eyes. Alison had the weirdest feeling that she was looking down into two deep wells with no bottom to them at all. Just then the seal gave a feeble jerk with its flippers, trying to raise itself up, but fell back weakly, panting.

"It looks like that seal's got into some oil and has come up to try and rub it off in the sand," Gareth said. "Now it's exhausted and can't get back to the sea."

"Oh, the poor thing! What can we do?"

"I'll pick it up and put it back where it belongs."

"Are you sure you'll be able to?" Alison asked, looking at the seal doubtfully. "It may be a baby, but it looks terribly heavy."

"Certainly I can," Gareth said confidently.

The thought crossed Alison's mind that he just might be showing off a little for her benefit. She suppressed a smile and moved forward to help him.

"Well," he said, just a shade less cheerfully, "here goes!" He leaned down to pick up the seal.

Alison leaned down as well and together they put their arms around it. It twisted suddenly in their grasp. Startled, Alison let go and jumped back.

"Er — do seals bite?" she asked dubiously.

"I should say they do," Gareth replied. "Here, let me do it. I can manage."

"No, I'll help." Alison gritted her teeth and stepped forward again.

They grabbed hold of it, but this time it twisted even more furiously and bit at them fiercely.

"Watch it, Alison!" Gareth shouted, jumping back. He made another grab for it. "I'll get it this time!" He caught the seal around the tail — as far away from those teeth as he could get — and managed to half lift it up, staggering under the weight. The seal lashed out furiously at him. There was no way Alison could get near it.

"Quick, Gareth. Drag it down to the water!" she screamed.

The seal, however, had very different ideas. It seemed to be getting livelier and kept twitching around, doing its very best to bite a piece out of this thing that was holding it in such an undignified manner. At the same time it was uttering short, sharp barks of outrage. Alison made one more try to help, then collapsed onto the sand, laughing.

Gareth kept on lurching towards the water, grunting and panting with the effort, trying not to let go but at the same time trying to keep out of biting range. Finally he reached the water's edge and collapsed into the waves. The seal landed on top of him and lay perfectly still for one startled moment. Then, with a thrust of its flippers, it disappeared under the waves. As they watched from shore, they saw the black speck of its head reappear in the foaming crash of water at the foot of the great cliff at the other end of the beach. Soon the tiny head was joined by another, and then another.

"That's the same old grand-da out there that's been bringing his family in here for years," Gareth said, still gasping. He pointed to one exceptionally large seal that had climbed out onto the rocks for a moment. When it dove back in, all the heads disappeared.

"They're beautiful," Alison said, staring at the spot where the seals had submerged. "I've never seen seals before. Out in the ocean, I mean," she added quickly. "Only in zoos. Do they come here often?"

"Oh yes," Gareth answered. "They're here all the time. I love to watch them whenever I come down." He looked at Alison, then quickly looked away again. "How *are* you liking Wales so far?" he asked. "I don't think I gave you a chance to answer before."

Alison was amazed to see that now he was blushing. Was he actually shy of *her*?

"I like it. Very much," she added quickly. Her voice hadn't sounded as definite as she'd meant it to.

"And the house? Are you getting on well there?"

Did she imagine it, or was there something funny about the way he had asked that question? She looked at him searchingly, but he had turned away from her again.

"It's — it's a strange old house, isn't it?" she answered. "Did you know my father's great-aunt when she lived there?"

"Not really. She was pretty old and kept to herself most of the time. My grandmam knew her, though."

There was something odd in the way he was speaking, Alison was sure of it. For a moment she hesitated, tempted to tell him about the room and the girl she had seen there, but she caught herself. She didn't know this boy at all, and he would certainly think she was crazy if she started talking about ghosts!

"You — you're just here for the summer then?" she asked, changing the subject abruptly. Gareth looked relieved. Why? What made him so uncomfortable about the cliff house?

"Yes," he answered. "I come down to help Meiriona out during the summers. I love Llanarfon," he added, enthusiasm brightening his face. "I don't think there could be a spot much more beautiful than this in the whole world."

Alison looked around her at the wide beach, at the waves breaking on the rocks around them, and agreed. Ottawa seemed very tame and far away compared with this wild scene. Then she remembered the cave and shivered involuntarily. But safe, she added to herself.

Gareth collected his towel and clothes and walked Alison back to the path that led up to their road. The cat followed unobtrusively behind, trying hard to look as if it were out for a walk by itself and not attached to them at all. At the top, before they reached the road, Gareth stopped.

"You don't have to go all the way up to the road to get home," he said. "You can cut across here along the top of the cliff and get to your back garden. It's much shorter."

"Oh. Thanks. I'll do that." Alison stood for an awkward moment, not sure what to say next.

"We live down the road," Gareth added. "In that white stone cottage just before the village."

"Oh! Where the old lady lives!" Alison blurted out before she could stop herself.

"Yes, that's right. That's my grandmam."

Alison remembered the way the old lady had stared after them. Suddenly there were goosebumps on her arms again.

"I come down to the beach quite often after the library closes," Gareth was saying. "Would you like to come and swim with me sometime?"

Alison hardly heard him. "Oh. Yes. All right," she said absently. "I'd love to," she added quickly, seeing the hurt look on his face.

"Super. I'll call by your house." He shouldered his towel and loped off down the road. A rustle in the bushes told her his cat was not far behind.

Alison headed back towards Pen-y-Craig. When she reached the high-walled back garden she stopped for a moment, wondering how she was going to get in without going around to the gate at the front. Then she noticed a small gate and pushed through it, threading her way through the overgrown maze of bushes and flowers towards the back door.

I can't believe Dad will make any order out of this in just one summer, she thought, looking around her. Still there was an untamed, unruly kind of beauty to it.

A flutter of white at one of the upstairs windows caught her eye. She looked towards it. It was the window of Bronwen's room. And standing there, staring down at her with a pale, indescribably sad face, was the same girl Alison had seen writing in the diary.

Bronwen!

5

The past reaches out

Alison stared back for one long, shocked moment, then she ran for the house. Once inside, she raced up the stairs and yanked open the door to Bronwen's room. The window was standing wide open and the breeze coming in off the sea ruffled the white curtains back and forth. There was no one there.

She sank down onto a small, cloth-covered piece of furniture and stared around her, stunned.

"Bronwen?" She whispered the name into the empty room. Silence. Broken only by the ever-present cries of the birds and the sound of the sea.

She should be scared — terrified. But for some reason all she could think of was the terrible sadness of the girl's face. What had happened? Why had Bronwen called *her*? And what was she supposed to do — what *could* she do?

Alison put her hand down absentmindedly and touched the piece of furniture on which she was sitting. Suddenly she became aware of it. It felt like a small stool of some sort. The vision she had had of Bronwen sitting, writing, came back to her and she remembered that she had been sitting on a stool. Alison jumped up and pulled the dustcloth off in one swift motion. There it was! Exactly as she had seen it! She turned to the other pieces of furniture and whipped the covers off them one after another. Disappointed, she stood looking at them. Nothing else was the same.

"Of course they wouldn't be," she muttered to herself. "Not after a hundred and seventy years."

But the stool was still there. Somehow or other it had managed to survive. Without really thinking about what she was doing, Alison picked it up and carried it over to the fireplace. She put it down in exactly the spot where she had seen it, then pulled at the loose brick. It came out easily this time. Holding the diary carefully in her hands, she sat down and opened it.

The 16th day of April in the year 1810.

I went walking on the beach today. Beaches, at least, are familiar to me. The tide was out and I discovered a huge cave in the cliffs right below our house.

Alison stared at the words. The cave! Bronwen had discovered the cave too! Eagerly she read on.

There are two enormous black rocks jutting out on either side of it and they look for all the world like the paws of some huge beast. Walking into the cave was frightening — it felt as if I were walking right between the paws into its mouth.

That's it, Alison thought. That's exactly how I felt.

When I came home, Morfudd, the village girl who comes in to help, told me that the fishermen call the cave Noddwr, the Protector. They say that smugglers used to use it for a hideaway sometimes. What a fearsome thought! I shall make it my own secret hiding place anyway. Somewhere only I know about where I can go when I want to be alone. I'll have that, at least.

The entry for that day ended there. Alison turned the page too quickly, and to her dismay a corner crumbled and fell to pieces. She forced her trembling fingers to slow down and be more careful. The next entry was smudged and very faint, and the light in the room was getting dim. Alison stood up and carried the fragile book over to the window. She didn't know if there was a lamp in this room — she hadn't seen one — but for some reason she didn't want to turn one on anyway. She squinted at the spidery handwriting.

The 18th day of April in the year 1810.
Catrin arrived today and I don't like her, just as I knew I wouldn't. The only consolation is that she is such a pale, wishy-washy looking thing I am sure to be able to do as I please with her. She's old too. Probably even over thirty. Much too old to get married now, so I suppose she considers herself lucky to be asked to come and live with us. She

41

*made a great pretense of liking me — to my disgust
she actually tried to kiss me on the cheek when we
were introduced. She even said that she liked the
house. This dreadful house! That surely betrayed
her false-heartedness. She's putting on a great pretense just to try to win my father and me over, but
I'll have none of it. I can see through her too easily
for that.*

*My father seems quite taken with her, however.
I couldn't believe he could ever be so foolish. He
smiled and laughed again for the first time since
my mother died. He even asked me, after Catrin had
retired to her room, if I didn't think she was
pleasant and pretty! She was so eager to impress
him that she offered to start lessons today — her
very first day here. I pretended to have a headache,
however, and was away from her within an hour.
As soon as I was free of her I slipped out the back
door and ran away. I went out across the cliff tops
until I reached Aberidris harbour, where I threw
myself down in the grass to watch the ships. There
were none there nearly so big and fine as my father's
and the others that sail into Aberystwyth, but it
made me feel better just to see them.*

The light was getting impossible. Alison low-
ered the book for a moment and gazed out the
window. There was a print of a lovely old ship
downstairs, with tall masts and full, billowing
sails. It must have been very like the one
Bronwen's father had captained. She closed her
eyes and tried to imagine what Aberidris harbour

must have looked like then. She and her father had passed by it on their way to the house and only fishing boats were there now — dirty looking things with smelly motors. How splendid it must have looked before, she thought, turning back to the diary with a sigh. She could hardly make out the writing at all now, but a strange sense of urgency made her read on.

As I gazed down into the water below I saw three specks and realized they were seals playing in the waves. They were having the most wonderful time diving and swimming, keeping right in where the water crashed against the rocks. One would think they would be dashed to pieces there, but they seemed to be entirely at ease. I haven't often seen seals before — Aberystwyth is a trace too far north for them — and I was enchanted with them.

I soon realized that I had stayed out far longer than I had intended and I would surely have been missed at home. I started to hurry back, but the thought that everybody would be worried about me slowed my steps. Let them worry, I thought. What do I care? When I finally did reach home it was almost dark and it gave me great satisfaction to hear my father tell Catrin she must not be so careless with me.

The room was so dark now that Alison was forced to stop reading. She closed the book and slowly crossed over to put it back in its hiding place.

What a disagreeable girl. And yet there had been such an odd look in her eyes as she had stared down at her. Almost a pleading look. What was it she wanted? And what did it have to do with Alison?

The next day at breakfast her father seemed distracted, not like his usual self at all. "I think I'll just walk into Llanarfon this morning," he said as they finished washing up the dishes. The tone of his voice was almost too casual.

Alison looked up. "Why? Did we forget to buy something?"

"Er, no. I just — just feel like some exercise, that's all."

"You're not going to get much writing done at this rate," she teased.

To her utter amazement her father's cheeks flushed. "I — I thought I'd drop in at the library. There are a couple of books I could use that they might have there."

"In Llanarfon? What could they possibly have there that would have anything to do with your novel?"

Alison stared at him, puzzled. Then a sudden thought struck her. Was it possible? Could it really be possible that all he wanted was to see Gareth's sister again? Of course not. The only women her bookish father had been interested in for as long as she could remember wore flat-heeled, sensible shoes and talked about Plato. She'd often teased him about it and he had always replied that the one thing he didn't have time for in his busy life was a "date." Besides, at his age the idea was ridiculous. He was in his forties, for heaven's sake! Alison dismissed the thought, laughing at herself for even thinking it.

For the rest of the morning she busied herself cleaning up the kitchen and organizing the cupboards. It wasn't something she enjoyed doing, but she needed to keep herself occupied. To keep her away from Bronwen's room and that diary! One side of her was consumed with curiosity about it and wanted to race upstairs and read more. The other side of her never wanted to set foot in that room again. She felt that she was being drawn into something totally beyond her understanding. Something strange . . . frightening . . . dangerous. It was all right in the clear, cold light of morning, down here in the kitchen, to tell herself sternly that she had just imagined she had seen Bronwen. The trouble was, she couldn't believe herself. It was too real! And yet, if she *had* seen her . . .

No! It wasn't possible.

Alison argued with herself all morning. It wasn't until lunchtime had come and gone that she suddenly realized her father hadn't come home. Where could he be? Surely nothing could have happened to him between here and Llanarfon, but it wasn't like him to be gone for so long with no explanation. She made two salads and put them in the refrigerator to wait. By three o'clock she gave in to her growling stomach and took hers out and ate it. By four o'clock she was standing by the front window watching the road anxiously.

When her father finally came striding towards the house she almost collapsed with relief.

She tore out and threw herself at him. He had been whistling and the sound was choked off with a gurgle.

"Whoof! What in the world? Alison, you nearly knocked me off my feet!" He turned suddenly serious and grabbed her shoulders. "There's nothing wrong, is there?"

"Nothing wrong! It's after four o'clock and I've been worried sick about you!"

"You've been worried about me? Since when have you ever kept tabs on me? Alison, get hold of yourself!"

Alison was shaking. She knew she was over-reacting, but she couldn't help it. "You said you were just going to be gone for a while. I was so worried!" she repeated. "I made a salad for you for lunch and you didn't come . . ."

"Oh, pet, I'm so sorry. I should have let you know somehow, I guess, but there isn't a phone. I met Meiriona Ellis at the library and she offered to show me around a bit. The library closes early on Saturdays. We had lunch at a very nice lunchroom in the village. Run by Mrs. Jones. You remember Mrs. Jones-the-Bakery? Then we went for a walk along the cliffs. Went as far as Aberidris. Great day! Marvellous air! I feel as healthy and spritely as a newborn lamb!"

"I *thought* you came here to write a book!" Alison shouted at him. "I *thought* you came here to work, not make a fool of yourself over someone young enough to be your daughter!"

Mr. Evans stared at Alison in shocked amazement. She bit her tongue, shocked herself at her outburst.

He was the first to recover. "Meiriona's not all that young, Alison, and all we did was have lunch and go for a walk. Don't you think you're exaggerating things a little? What's the matter with you anyway?"

Alison stared back at him miserably. She didn't know what was the matter. She couldn't remember ever having yelled at him like that before. She opened her mouth to apologize, but before she could get the words out, her father went on.

"She's a remarkable woman, actually. Took her Master's at the University at Aberystwyth and was all set to go on for her Ph.D. when both her parents were killed in a car crash three years ago. Her brother's quite a bit younger than she, and there was no one to look after him or her old grandmother, so she just chucked everything and came back here to take care of them. Remarkable! You don't see that kind of family devotion much anymore. And she doesn't even think much of it. She says she's lucky because her job at the library lets her carry on with her studies on her own. Remarkable!"

If he says "remarkable" once more I'm going to scream, Alison thought. All ideas of apologizing had evaporated. "Well," she said angrily, "I guess you can have the salad for supper. I'm going to the beach." She turned and flounced out of the room.

She changed into her bathing suit, threw on a

jacket and started back down the stairs. Outside the door to Bronwen's room she paused for a second. The urge to go in and read more of the diary was strong. Then she shrugged angrily and turned away. She had problems enough of her own — she was in no mood to put up with Bronwen's.

It wasn't until she was halfway to the beach path that she realized the sun had gone in and the day had turned cold and windy. On an impulse she started to follow the path that led along the cliff-tops. She was so immersed in her own thoughts she didn't notice at first just how far she was going, until suddenly she came to a harbour — Aberidris harbour. This must be the very spot where Bronwen sat and watched the seals and the ships, she thought, startled.

Bronwen again! Was there no escaping her? The wind whipped and tore at her, but she scarcely felt it. She stared out at the harbour, but the harbour she was seeing in her mind was not the one that actually lay before her. It was a harbour filled with tall, proud ships, their sails straining in the wind.

6

They felt the doom

The next day was Sunday. Alison came down to breakfast feeling drugged. She hadn't slept well, tossing and turning until well after midnight. When she had finally fallen asleep she'd had strange, uneasy dreams. Bronwen's voice had called and called. Alison had searched for her along endless corridors and everywhere in the room, which seemed to have grown to enormous proportions. But somehow the voice had stayed just out of reach, Bronwen herself just out of sight.

Alison poured milk over her cereal and set it in front of her, then sat there, forgetting to eat.

"Well, Alison," her father said heartily, "what would you say to going to church today?"

At first she didn't react, then the meaning of his words hit her. Another shock. She couldn't remember the last time her father had gone to church. What was happening to him anyway?

The mystery was explained by his next words. "Meiriona suggested we go. It's a lovely little village church, she says, and the vicar is a lively man who preaches an interesting sermon. I thought we might just drop in. It's only a short walk from here."

Alison's first impulse was to refuse, but she changed her mind. The thought of church was somehow appealing.

The grey stone church, high up on the cliffs overlooking the town of Aberidris and the harbour, looked very old. Meiriona was waiting for them by the front door. Alison felt an unexpected surge of pleasure when she saw Gareth standing beside her. She smiled at him, remembering his struggle with the seal, and he grinned back. He looked oddly stiff and formal in a jacket and tie. Alison was glad she had fought her unruly curls into submission and tied them back neatly for a change.

The service was simple and quiet. As Alison relaxed back into the pew and listened to the small choir sing, she began to feel more peaceful then she had since the day they'd arrived. But her happy, contented mood was shattered when Meiriona leaned towards her father and whispered something to him. Mr. Evans smiled down at her with a look on his face and a sparkle in his eyes that Alison couldn't ever remember seeing before. She looked away quickly and didn't respond when Gareth held out his prayer book to share with her. She paid no attention at all to the rest of the service, fidgeting during the vicar's sermon and longing only to be out and away from there. Away from Meiriona.

When Meiriona and her father lingered to talk to the vicar, Alison walked away from them and leaned on a low stone fence that enclosed a small graveyard.

"Most of my ancestors lie in there," Gareth said, coming up quietly behind her.

She started. She had forgotten about him.

"Oh," she replied noncommittally. Her mind was too full of the picture of Meiriona and her father bending towards each other to pay much attention to what he was saying. Then a thought struck her. "This church must be very old, I guess," she said.

"It is that," Gareth answered. "Look. There's an inscription by the door." He led Alison over to inspect the cornerstone by the front door. Carved there she read: *Rebuilt in 1849.*

If it was rebuilt in 1849, then it must have been there for a long time before that. Maybe even when Bronwen was alive . . .

"Is it the only church around here?" she asked.

"Yes, it is. Always has been as far as I know."

Then Bronwen had probably walked along the clifftop path to this very church. Everything she did, I'm doing now, Alison thought. Everywhere she went, I'm going too. The last of the comfort she had felt in church disappeared. She was frightened. Really and truly frightened. What had happened to Bronwen? What was going to happen to *her*?

Some of what she was feeling must have shown on her face, because Gareth looked at her curiously. "Is anything the matter, Alison?" he asked.

"No, nothing," she answered shortly. She was

thinking of the diary. She must get back and read the rest of it. She had to find out —

"Alison, Meiriona's invited us to drop by their cottage and meet her grandmother on our way home," Mr. Evans called out as he and Meiriona came up to join them. They were laughing happily together. Alison winced as she saw what an attractive couple they made. Her father, with his waving dark hair and almost black eyes, looked as Welsh as Meiriona. Alison had inherited her blondish, almost red hair and grey-green eyes from her mother.

"Why don't you two go on ahead and we'll follow in a few minutes," Meiriona said in her light, musical voice. "There are some friends here I'd like to introduce to your father," she added, smiling at Alison.

Alison didn't smile back. Who did she think she was anyway, telling her what to do? To make matters worse, Meiriona hooked her arm light-heartedly through Mr. Evans' and turned him away before Alison could even answer. He walked off without looking back.

Like a tame dog, she thought viciously.

"Come on, Alison," Gareth said enthusiastically. "Would you like to go swimming again this afternoon? It's a great day for it. Maybe we'll rescue a few more seals!"

There was no way she could refuse gracefully.

As they walked towards the cottage, Gareth chattered on companionably, but Alison only half listened to him. His mentioning the seals had reminded her of the cave.

"How did you know which cave I meant?" she blurted out suddenly, interrupting him.

He stopped talking and stared at her.

"Yesterday," Alison went on. "When I told you I had nearly been trapped in a cave, you said, 'That cave,' as if you knew right away which one it was."

For a moment he didn't answer her. Then he spoke slowly, cautiously, as if searching for the right words. As if afraid he might say too much, or say something wrong. "Well — you mentioned the cat. I know which cave my cat goes in . . ." He sounded as if he didn't expect her to believe him, and she didn't.

"But you started to say something else, that I shouldn't something. Shouldn't what? What is there about that cave anyway?"

"I don't want to repeat silly stories that might worry you. And they *are* only silly stories — believe me."

"Who are you trying to convince?" Alison retorted. "Me or you?" She stopped in her tracks and turned to face him full on. "There is something special about that cave, isn't there? I know. I felt it."

"You felt what?" Gareth interrupted quickly.

"I don't know what I felt. I just felt something — something *wrong*."

"The tide was coming in. You were frightened . . ."

Alison almost stamped her foot in frustration. "Tell me the truth, Gareth. What is wrong with that cave? How did you know where I'd been? Why did you look so upset when I first saw you?"

Gareth drew a deep breath. He seemed to come to a decision. "I don't know why I was so upset. No, really," he added quickly as Alison grimaced impatiently. "I've known about that cave all my life, and I've never liked it, but I've never had such a bad feeling about it before. Even before I actually saw you. I was walking along the beach when I suddenly felt something dreadful in the air. Then I saw you climbing over the point and you looked so desperate. I knew right then where you'd been, even before you told me about the cat. Don't ask me how, but I knew." His voice trailed off.

Alison felt a tremor go down her spine. "I suppose the cave is haunted," she said lightly, trying to make a joke of it. But her voice wavered in the middle of the sentence.

To her surprise, Gareth didn't deny it. Instead he just kept standing there staring at her strangely.

"You're in danger here," he said. Then he shook himself brusquely, as if to wake himself up. "Hark at me," he laughed. "Pay me no mind. I don't know what's come over me. It's listening to my grandmam's stories too much, that's what does it. But the cave," he went on, forestalling any attempt she might make to say anything further, "of course it's haunted! All good Welsh caves are haunted. And that one most of all. After all, it was used by smugglers in the olden days and has probably seen more than its share of evil deeds. If you must hear about it, then you shall." His tone was lighthearted and joking now, deliberately mocking his own words and demanding that she mock them with him.

He turned on his heel resolutely, and for the rest of the way to the cottage regaled her with tale after tale of smugglers, shipwrecks, foul deeds and ghosts, each one more unbelievable than the last. He allowed her no chance to speak seriously again, and by the time they reached his home she was laughing in spite of herself.

"Here we are at the cottage, then. Let's just pop in and meet Grandmam. She'll be glad to see a new face."

Gareth took Alison by the arm and led her through the gate. Roses grew on one side of the low front door, and a honeysuckle vine almost overpowered the other.

"Mind the wasps," he warned cheerfully as they ducked their heads to go in. "That honeysuckle does bring them round, but it's Grandmam's pride and joy, so it's worth it."

It took Alison's eyes a moment to get used to the cool darkness inside the cottage after the sunlight. Then she made out the figure of a tiny old lady sitting in a chair in the corner of the room. The room was neat and clean, with whitewashed walls and bright curtains at the windows. A stone fireplace held a mantel where a pair of china dogs growled ferociously at each other from either end, and various brass and copper ornaments shone dully. Gareth's cat was stretched out between the dogs, oblivious of their snarls.

"Grandmam, this is Alison Evans." Gareth spoke loudly to get the old lady's attention. "She and her father have come to live at Pen-y-Craig for the summer."

"The last of the Evans have finally come back to Cliff House, have they?" the old lady said in a weary, cracked voice. "Well, good luck to you is all I can say. You'll be needing it, living in such an unhappy place."

"Now, Grandmam," Gareth chided, "don't be saying things like that." He turned to Alison. "She's just old," he said in a whisper, "and she gets fancies. You mustn't pay any attention to her."

But Alison was staring at the old lady. She knew something about Pen-y-Craig! "Why do you call it an unhappy place?" she asked urgently. "What happened there?"

"She's just talking, Alison," Gareth interrupted, looking worried. "Don't go taking what I was saying about ghosts and things too seriously, now."

"What do *you* know about ghosts at Pen-y-Craig?" Alison asked, turning on him quickly. But before he could answer, the old lady had gone on.

"An unhappy place," she repeated. "Everyone who's ever lived there has been unhappy." She pointed a bony, shaking finger at Alison. "They felt it," she added. "They all felt it, and you will too."

"Felt what?" Alison's throat was dry and the words came out raggedly. It was as if that bony finger was pointing a sliver of ice right into her heart.

56

The old lady's voice sank low. Alison strained to hear her. She couldn't understand the words at all, though, and realized Gareth's grandmother must be speaking Welsh.

"What did she say?" Alison begged desperately, turning to Gareth. "Please. What did she say?" Then shivers cascaded down her back as the old lady repeated her words in English.

"They felt the doom," she said, rocking herself back and forth. "They felt the doom."

"Oh, for heaven's sake, Grandmam, you're scaring poor Alison half to death," Gareth burst out. "What about old Mrs. Evans? She lived there, didn't she?"

The old lady shut her mouth in a firm line. Then, slowly, she said, "There's things we old people know about that we wish we didn't. At the end she couldn't bear it either. You know that, Gareth." Then she shut her mouth tightly again and wouldn't say anything more. Even when Meiriona brought Mr. Evans in and introduced him, she just shut her eyes and pretended to sleep. Finally Meiriona gave up in exasperation.

"I'm sorry," she apologized. "I'd never have invited you in if I'd known she was going to be in one of her moods. Please excuse her."

They had their tea anyway, but the atmosphere was strained. Alison was perversely glad that her father seemed uneasy and anxious to be away.

Gareth followed them to the gate when they left. "Do you still want to go swimming this afternoon?"

"Yes, of course."

He went on quickly, in a low voice that the others couldn't hear. "Please don't worry about what my grandmam said. She really does imagine things, you know. She's so very old now."

His eyes sought Alison's and held them intently. They were the same dark eyes as his grandmother's. For a moment Alison was startled by the similarity. She felt a wave of confusion overwhelm her. Gareth's uneasiness about the cave . . . his grandmother's ominous words . . . Bronwen . . . What was real? What was her imagination?

"Thanks again for the tea," Mr. Evans was saying to Meiriona. He turned to Alison. "Come on, we'd better get home and let these people have their Sunday dinner." He had recovered his normal good humour as soon as they were out of the house and away from old Mrs. Ellis.

"See you later, then," Gareth called after them as they began to walk away. "About four o'clock. Shall I come by your house?"

"All right," Alison called back. She turned to follow her father, her mind spinning in circles. Should she tell Gareth about Bronwen? He'd had the same bad feelings about the cave as she had, and he seemed to know something about Pen-y-Craig. Surely he would believe her. Surely he wouldn't laugh at her.

7
A warning

After she and her father had eaten a quick lunch, Alison flew up the stairs to Bronwen's room, all hesitation gone. Curiosity — and something even stronger than that — had won out over fear. She *had* to find out what had happened to Bronwen.

Her father had already shut himself in his room, and she could hear the typewriter clacking away furiously. With her heart pounding, she pulled the now familiar brick out and sank down onto the stool to read.

The 29th day of April in the year 1810.

A ship came into Aberidris today bringing limestone and coal. Father told us about it last night. Morfudd was still here and said that all the villagers would turn out and there would be gaiety and amusements on the beach. She said it was always an event that everyone looked forward to, and she was very excited. The ship arrived when Catrin and I were doing our lessons and she, silly thing that she is, was in such haste to go and see it that she finished the lessons early without my even asking. She wanted me to go as well, but I was certainly not going to mix with a crowd of villagers on the beach!

After she left, however, the house seemed very lonely. Morfudd hadn't even bothered to come in, and I had no idea where father could be. I kept wondering just what was going on down in the harbour, and finally my curiosity was too much for me. I ran out of the house, glad to have an excuse to leave it behind, and made my way over the cliffs as quickly as I could to the spot where I had watched the seals playing.

I arrived panting and out of breath just as the ship was coming in on the tide. She sailed in as far as possible and anchored — there is no place to dock here. Then a great shout went up for porters. All the men who live in the cottages along the beach came streaming out as soon as they heard the call. I was utterly amazed when, after boarding the ship, they immediately commenced throwing blocks of limestone and lumps of coal off her and into the water! I couldn't understand it at all until much later. By the time the ship was unloaded, the tide was going out, and as it receded and the ship sailed out again with it, the lumps of limestone and coal were left sitting on the wet sand. All the men had to do then was walk back out and bring them up onto the beach.

It was very late by this time and on the beach the pale blue flames of the kilns were burning brightly. I remembered Morfudd telling us that the kilns are lit and kept burning until the shipping season is over. The men started getting very silly then, wagering with each other to see who could lift and carry the biggest stones. Suddenly I saw a familiar figure and was mortified to realize that it was my own father. He seemed to be enjoying himself hugely and I'm sure he was trying to impress Catrin who was right there watching. He's much too old for that sort of thing — one would think he'd remember his dignity!

I was so disgusted and humiliated that I was about to turn away, but then they started breaking the limestone up into little pieces and putting it into the kilns. It burns into a powder, Morfudd said, then they mix it with water and use it for mortar to hold stones together when building. The women were scurrying around collecting shellfish and stuffing them into the cracks of the kilns to bake. Catrin was helping as well, having forgotten her dignity just as thoroughly as my father.

It was dark by then and very cold. The smell of the baking crayfish wafted up to where I lay hidden and I suddenly realized how hungry I was. There were several children dancing around to keep warm while they waited for the shellfish to bake, and it all looked so happy and inviting I was tempted to go down and join them. Then I saw my father and Catrin standing a little apart from the others and laughing together. Such a pain twisted inside my chest that I could hardly breathe, and in spite of myself I started to cry.

I turned away and went home, stumbling in the dark and trying to wipe away all trace of tears so

*that no one should see. I needn't have worried,
however, as no one was here when I arrived — not
even Morfudd. She's down at the beach as well, I
suppose. All I could find in the kitchen was some
cold meat and bread, and I have brought it up here
to my room to eat as I write this. Father and Catrin
are not home yet. I don't care, though. If they want to
amuse themselves in such a rude, rough way they
may. I certainly shan't.*

To Alison's dismay, many of the next pages
were so torn and faded she could only make out a
word here and there. The next legible entry was for
almost a month later.

The 20th day of May in the year 1810.
    *It's Sunday and we've just walked back from
church at Aberidris.*

The same church, Alison thought. I knew it
would be! She read on.

*I've been sent up here as punishment for being rude
to Catrin. As usual she and my father simpered and
laughed together all the way to and from church,
hardly even noticing that I was there as well. When
we returned she was bold enough to ask me to run
and fetch her shawl for her! "Ask Morfudd," I said
to her. "I'm not your servant." And I turned my back
to her.*
    *What a fuss! You would think I had struck her.
She immediately burst into tears, ninny that she is,*

and my father was furious. I've never heard him roar at me in such a fashion, and all because of her. It's clear to see who's most important now in this house. It hasn't taken her long at all to ferret her way into the running of everything around here. I hate her! She still pretends to like me no matter what I do, but I know it's all sham. All she wants is my father, and to be mistress of this house, but I won't let her. I'll find some way of stopping her — of getting rid of her forever.

A knock on the half-open door interrupted her reading.

"Alison, are you in there?" her father called. "Gareth's here."

"Coming," she called back. Quickly she hid the book again and went to the door.

"Oh, good. You've been cleaning up in here," her father said, looking around at the uncovered furniture. "Looks like the inside of an antique store, doesn't it?"

Alison brushed past him. "Tell Gareth I'll be right down," she said. "I'll just get changed."

Her mind was made up. She would tell Gareth all about the diary and everything she had seen since they'd arrived. He might laugh at her, but she remembered the uneasy look in his eyes that morning and she was sure he wouldn't. If there was anyone around here who would believe her, it would be him. Maybe he could tell her some things about this house too. Maybe now she could get some answers.

But when she went downstairs to meet him she saw Meiriona standing beside him with a large wicker picnic hamper. "I thought I'd fix a picnic supper to eat on the beach," she said cheerfully. "To make up for our grandmam being so inhospitable this morning, do you know. I hope you like cold chicken."

"Love it!" answered Mr. Evans, who had come down behind Alison. She saw that he, too, had changed into his bathing suit. "This is a great idea, Meiriona." Taking the basket from her, he led the way out. Alison followed with Gareth, her face stormy.

When they reached the beach they found a sheltered spot under the rocks and spread out their towels. Mr. Evans immediately challenged Meiriona to a race into the waves. As she watched them run laughing into the water, Alison's face became even stormier.

"It's ridiculous," she muttered. "He's acting like a fool!"

"Your dad and my sister certainly get along well together, don't they?" Gareth remarked. He either hadn't heard her or chose to pretend that he hadn't.

She didn't answer. She was staring at the two figures splashing each other in the waves.

"I'm glad to see Meiriona meet someone she likes," Gareth went on, oblivious of her stony silence. "She doesn't have any friends here — men friends, I mean. You know, that she can talk to or go out with. Everybody is either too old for her or too young — or too scared of her brains!"

"Well, my father is certainly too old for her!" Alison burst out. "I can't *believe* the way he's acting! He's never acted like this before!"

"But doesn't he go out? Date?"

"*Date*? My *father*?" Alison made the word "date" sound like something unbelievable. "He's much too old for that kind of nonsense."

"But isn't he lonely? I mean, it is a long time since your mother died, isn't it?" Gareth asked gently.

"Of course he's not lonely. He's got me."

"But you've got friends, haven't you?" he persisted.

"Yes, of course. But that's different. Daddy's got his work, and his novel. He's too busy. And he's certainly never gone out with anyone like Meiriona!" She flushed a little as she realized how rude her words sounded. "I mean — well, Meiriona's so much younger than he is . . ."

"Not all that much, although I always call her my *old* sister," Gareth said, laughing. "It makes her furious." Then he added in a teasing voice, "It sounds to me as if you just don't want to share him. You want your dad all to yourself."

Alison flushed even more hotly. "That's not true!" She jumped up, ready to run away from him, but he reached up and caught her hand.

"Look," he said, "I'm sorry. Let's forget it. Shall we raid the basket before they come back, or have a swim too?"

Alison glared down at him, struggling to get her hand away from his, but he got to his feet and began pulling her towards the sea.

"Swim," he shouted, deciding the question for her.

She still pulled back. She'd suddenly remembered her resolve to tell him about Bronwen. Her father and Meiriona were well out of earshot — this would be the perfect time for it. But Gareth gave her no choice. He tugged her down to the water's edge and threw himself into the waves. Besides, Alison was still too angry to talk.

But she found it impossible to stay mad at Gareth for very long. Soon she was enjoying herself after all. By the time they had swum and finished their picnic supper, the sun was low on the horizon. It was getting cold very quickly and Alison pulled on a sweater. Her father lit a small brush fire on the beach and they all huddled around it.

Alison threw a branch onto the fire, then looked around her. "By the way," she said to Gareth as he, too, added wood to the fire, "where's your cat today?"

"He was busy at a mousehole when I left. I'll bet he was furious when he realized I'd gone without him."

"What does he do in the winter when you're away at school?"

"Oh, he keeps my grandmam company," Gareth answered.

The mention of the old lady brought Alison's mind sharply back to Bronwen and the mystery of Pen-y-Craig. There had been no further opportunity to ask Gareth about it, or about what the old lady had meant. For a while, as they had been swimming and eating their supper, she had even forgotten it. Now it all came flooding back. "They felt the doom," the old lady had said.

But there was no chance to ask about it then. Not with Meiriona and her father sitting right there. And later, when they had put out the fire, tidied up and started back up the path to the house, she still did not find a chance to talk to him.

As they said goodbye where their paths separated, Alison managed to draw Gareth aside. "Will you be swimming tomorrow after you finish work?" she asked.

"I won't be here. I have to go back to Aberystwyth to pick up some things I left at school," he explained.

"Oh." Alison was dismayed. She hadn't realized how much she'd been counting on him. "Will you be gone long?"

"Just a day or two."

"I — I wanted to tell you something," she began hesitantly. "And ask you — ask you about what your grandmother said this morning."

"You mustn't pay any attention to her."

"But — but there *is* something — something at Pen-y-Craig . . ."

"Have you seen anything? Heard anything?" Gareth almost snapped the questions at her.

Alison looked at him in surprise. "I can't explain now. It's too complicated." She glanced around her desperately. Her father was coming towards them. "When you get back . . ."

Mr. Evans swung a heavy arm around her shoulders. "Goodnight, Meiriona. Goodnight, Gareth," he boomed.

"Alison! Be care—"

The rest of what Gareth had been going to say was cut off as Mr. Evans went on. "Thanks for the picnic. See you tomorrow, Meiriona."

Had Gareth been going to say "Be careful"? His eyes met Alison's as Meiriona called her goodbyes, and Alison was sure he was trying to relay a message to her.

A warning?

8
A plea ignored

Alison woke the next morning with a sense of loss
and depression. For a moment she couldn't think
why, then she remembered: Gareth was leaving.
True, he would be gone for only a few days, but she
had been counting on him to help her make sense
of this whole business. Help her decide what to do.
As she lay in bed and tried to muster enough
energy to get up, she thought briefly of going to her
father and telling him. She could show him the
diary as proof that Bronwen existed. Had existed,
she corrected herself quickly.

But he won't believe me, she thought hopelessly. Of course he won't believe me. He'll think
finding the diary was just a coincidence and that
I've been imagining things because of it. Besides,
right now he's far more interested in Meiriona
than in my problems. How could he get so involved
with somebody in such a short time? We've only
been here five days, for heaven's sake!

For that matter, how could I get so involved
with a diary in only five days? And with Bronwen.
With a — a *ghost*! The thought pushed itself into

her mind. Along with it came a strange, unwelcome sense of urgency. A feeling that time was running out.

Alison shook her head angrily and went downstairs on leaden feet.

At breakfast her father announced cheerfully that he was going to work in the morning and then drop by the library to see Meiriona for lunch. Alison didn't bother answering him. For a moment he looked at her, a worried frown creasing his forehead.

"You don't mind, do you? I mean — you won't be lonely, will you?"

He sounded a little guilty, but Alison was too immersed in her own thoughts to care. "No, of course not," she answered. "I'll go down to the beach."

But she didn't. The moment she heard her father's typewriter start up, she headed for Bronwen's room. It was the last place she wanted to go, but again there was that sense that she *had* to do it. She *had* to find out what Bronwen wanted.

As soon as she went in she could feel an unbearable tension. The room was charged with the feeling. It sent prickles along her arms and shivers down her back. She looked around nervously, but everything seemed the same. The wind was rattling the windowpane as usual, accentuating the emptiness of the room. And yet more strongly than ever before she felt that someone else was in there with her.

Alison retrieved the diary and opened it to the

last entry she had read, then turned the page. The next entry was illegible. It had been stained with something — probably the damp — and was a faded and mildewed mess. She turned another page. To her dismay it was the same. She leafed through the pages desperately, but aside from a word here and there, she couldn't make out any of the writing. What if there were no more legible entries at all? Then, suddenly, she came upon a page with a clear date at the top. With a sigh of relief, she started to read.

The 4th day of July in the year 1810.

 Summer is well upon us now and matters grow worse and worse. Catrin and my father have joined solidly against me. He upholds her all the time and never sides with me at all. In the evenings they sit comfortably together while I am left out completely. Catrin pretends to be so sweet and loving to me, but it is false. I know it and I won't be deceived.

 As I write this I can see the sails of a large ship plying up the coast, making for Aberystwyth, I imagine. To my home. Soon they, too, will stop. After the summer draws to a close the shipping season will be over for the year. I'll do something to end this misery before then — I promise I will.

Again the writing became blurred and impossible to read. Frustrated, Alison searched through the rest of the book, trying hard to be careful of the brittle pages but desperate to read more. She looked up, startled by the abrupt silence. The wind had died down completely. Her uneasiness grew. She stood up and put the book back into its hiding place, her desire to read overcome by an inexplicable fear. What had happened to the wind? Why was everything so still?

Help me, Alison. Please help me.

It was the faintest of whispers, but it rang through the eerily silent room.

Alison whirled around, pressing herself against the rough bricks of the fireplace. There at the window, her face pale, her black hair falling loosely down her back, stood Bronwen.

"Bronwen!" Alison whispered, panic tightening her chest so she could hardly breathe.

I've waited so long . . . You're the only one . . .

Even as the voice spoke, the figure wavered and began to grow dim. "Don't go!" Alison cried. "Bronwen, don't go!"

But the girl had disappeared. Alison stood still for a moment, too stunned to move. Then she ran to the window, to the spot where Bronwen had stood.

"Bronwen," she called again to the emptiness.

There was only silence.

Then a sudden, wild gust of wind blew the window open with a crash. The heavy wooden frame caught Alison squarely on the forehead. She fell without a sound and lay unmoving while the wind fought and tore at the billowing curtains above her.

When she came back to consciousness her father was bending over her, holding a cool wet cloth on her forehead. "That's a nasty bump you've got there," he said. He was obviously trying to make his voice light, but the colour had drained from his face and there were deep lines around his mouth that Alison had never noticed before. "How are you feeling?"

She tried to sit up, but fell back as the room swam around her. "Dizzy," she replied.

"Just lie there and rest for a minute," her father advised. "How in the world did this happen?"

"The wind," she answered weakly. "I was standing by the window and the wind blew it open. I guess it hit me."

"Stupid old windows, opening inwards," her father muttered. "Just take it easy now. As soon as you're feeling well enough I'll head for the village and bring back a doctor."

"No!" Alison sat up again, ignoring the dizziness. She grabbed her father's arm desperately. "No! Don't leave me alone. Please!"

Gently her father pushed her back down. "Take it easy," he said again, alarmed. "It's all right, Alison. I won't leave you until I'm sure you're all right, but you must have a doctor."

It was late in the evening, however, before he was able to bring the doctor, who assured them that no serious damage seemed to have been done. "Still," he said as he turned to leave, "I'd pop her round to the hospital for a few X-rays in the morning, Mr. Evans, if I were you. Just to be sure, you know. And keep her quiet for a few days. The more rest the better."

The X-rays were normal, but Mr. Evans took

the doctor seriously and insisted that Alison stay in bed for the next two days. She had such a headache that she didn't really object. Besides, it was a good way to avoid Bronwen's room and Bronwen's diary. She didn't feel up to facing that.

But there was no way to avoid thinking about Bronwen. And this time there was no way to avoid the fact that she *had* seen her. And *spoken* to her. But what was it Bronwen wanted to tell her? How could *she* help? How could this possibly be happening? The questions spun around and around in Alison's aching head until she almost cried.

Mr. Evans waited on Alison and nursed her constantly for the next two days, but her mind was in too much of a turmoil to appreciate it. She couldn't even summon up enough interest to joke with him about his cooking. He began looking more and more worried. Finally, on the afternoon of the second day, he came in and sat on the edge of her bed. She had been holding a book, but had not really been reading.

"Alison," he began, "what's the matter? You're not acting like yourself at all. The doctor says you're all right — what is it?"

"It's nothing, Dad. Really. I just have a headache."

"But there *is* something. I've never seen you like this. And there's another thing. I didn't want to ask you until you were feeling better, but I couldn't help wondering. What were you doing in that room anyway? It seems to me that you spend a lot of time in there. And it seems to me that there's something bothering you. Is there a connection?"

Alison sighed. Her father knew her too well. She raised her eyes and looked at him. It would be such a relief to tell him. What did it matter if he didn't believe her? Just telling him would help. She opened her mouth to speak, but before she could get the words out, the doorbell rang.

Her father's face brightened immediately. "That'll be Meiriona," he said. "She was so worried about you. She dropped around yesterday but you were asleep. Hold on a minute and I'll go let her in. She'll brighten you up."

Alison shut her mouth abruptly and sank back down into the bed. "I don't want to see her," she said shortly.

"But she came just to see you," her father objected.

"I can hardly believe *that*," Alison answered bitterly. "I've got a headache, Dad. It hurts. You talk to her. I'd rather rest."

"Are you sure?"

She nodded.

"Okay, then. I'll be up with supper as soon as she's left and we can talk." With a final pat on her shoulder he fairly bounced out of the room.

But by the time he came up with her supper Alison had made up her mind. There was no point in talking to him. He would never believe her. And worse than that, he might even tell Meiriona and they'd both think she was weird. No. There was only one thing to do. The next morning, before she even tried to decipher any more of the diary, she

75

would go and talk to Mrs. Ellis. She knew something. Alison would ask her — beg her, if necessary — to tell her what had happened at Pen-y-Craig.

It took quite an argument with her father before he let her out the next morning, but Alison persisted. "I feel much better, Dad. Really I do," she insisted. "My headache is gone and all I need is a bit of fresh air. A short walk will be good for me."

"I'll go with you then," Mr. Evans said.

"Dad, you haven't done any work at all on your novel since I got that bump, have you? Be honest."

"Well, no," he admitted.

"Then I'll feel better if you work on it now. I'm fine. Believe me."

Her father looked tempted and finally gave in. "Okay," he agreed reluctantly. "But don't be gone too long."

"I won't. I promise." Alison was out the door before he could change his mind.

It was only a short walk to the cottage, but the closer she got to it, the more her steps slowed. What would she say to the old lady? How would she ask her? How would she even get in the cottage, for that matter? Gareth was away and Meiriona would be at the library. What if old Mrs. Ellis was inside and didn't hear her knocking? Could she just walk in?

When she finally reached the cottage and summoned up enough courage to rap on the door, however, it wasn't old Mrs. Ellis who answered. It was Meiriona, and she had obviously been crying.

"Meiriona! What's the matter?"

"It's Grandmam. She died last night in her sleep. The doctor's in there now."

"Oh, Meiriona, I'm so sorry!" Alison reached out instinctively to Meiriona, but at the same time, in spite of herself, she was thinking: Now I'll never find out. Unless I can find some more legible pages in the diary, or unless Gareth does know something, I'll never find out.

Gareth returned from Aberystwyth that same day. The funeral arrangements were simple. Mrs. Ellis would be buried in the same little churchyard where the rest of Gareth and Meiriona's family were, beside their parents.

During the next week Alison hardly saw her father alone at all. He was with Meiriona constantly — helping with the funeral arrangements, keeping her company, comforting her. The death of old Mrs. Ellis had upset Alison strangely, more than it should have. She was almost convinced now that she would never find the solution to the mystery of Pen-y-Craig. But for the time being, at least, it was a relief to push Bronwen and the diary out of her mind. She did what she could to help Gareth and Meiriona.

The church service was short, but very moving. Everyone in the village had come. Everyone had known and respected the old lady. As the choir sang a final hymn and they moved out into the churchyard, Alison found her eyes filling with tears. Death seemed so final. So frightening.

Meiriona saw her and put an arm around her comfortingly. "It's all right, Alison," she said. "She was a very old lady who lived a long and contented life. And she was very tired. It's much worse when people die too young." Her voice caught for a moment.

Alison knew she must be thinking of her own parents. Impulsively she put an arm around Meiriona as well. At that moment she felt a wave of sympathy and affection for her.

But sympathy, affection, and all other friendly feelings towards Meiriona were jolted out of her by the shock of her father's words the next evening. They had finished dinner and were sitting quietly together for the first time since Mrs. Ellis had died. "I've been talking to Meiriona about her future," Mr. Evans said.

Alison looked up quickly. "What do you mean?" she asked. A feeling of apprehension began to sneak up on her.

"Well, she's got much too fine a mind to be buried here in Llanarfon," he replied. "And now that old Mrs. Ellis is gone and Gareth is a little older, there's no need for her to stay. She'd find excellent professors and resources in her particular field at Ottawa University, so I've suggested she apply and plan to return with us in the fall. Gareth could still come and visit her on holidays," he added quickly. "He could even come permanently if he wished. It seems she's been left quite well off and there would be no problem with that."

"Meiriona? Come to Canada?" Alison asked incredulously. "Why? Why in the world would you suggest that? What do you care about where she studies or what she does?"

Mr. Evans stood up. He looked at Alison. "It seems I do care, Alison," he said. "It seems I do care very much what Meiriona does."

Alison stared at him in disbelief.

Her father turned to look out the window. "I thought I never would care for another woman after your mother died. I had you. I had my work, plenty of friends. My life seemed very complete and full. But now I've met Meiriona. I know it doesn't sound logical — I've known her such a short time. But I find that I can't face the thought of saying goodbye to her. Of her not being part of my life. Of our lives, Alison."

"Well, she won't be a part of *my* life!" Alison exploded. "We've been so happy! We don't need anyone else!"

"Yes, we do. I do. And in time you will too." Mr. Evans spoke gently and made a move towards Alison, but she jumped up and ran to the door.

"If you think I'm going to stay here for the rest of the summer and watch you and Meiriona — knowing that you . . ." She couldn't bring herself to say "care about her," much less "love her," which she supposed was what he meant. "I want to go home! I hate this place anyway. I want to go back to Canada. Right away." She was fighting the urge to cry. She wouldn't give him that satisfaction.

"You can't mean that, Alison. Where would you stay?"

"With Gran in Toronto. You know she offered

to let me stay there in the first place."

"But you said you didn't want to. That you'd rather come here with me."

"Well, now I want to."

Mr. Evans tried again. "Alison, please. I don't want you to go home. Let's just sleep on it tonight and we'll talk about it in the morning. Maybe you'll feel differently then."

"I won't," she answered. "I want out. I want away from here as quickly as possible. This is all Meiriona's fault," she threw in bitterly. "She's deliberately stolen you away from me."

"That's nonsense, Alison," her father said sharply. "I'm not yours to steal anyway. Any more than you are mine!" He sounded as furious as Alison.

But Alison wasn't listening to him. She had made up her mind. She never wanted to see Meiriona again.

And way back in that corner of her mind that was always telling her things she didn't want to hear, a small voice was adding: "And if you go home you'll never have to see Bronwen or think of her again either!"

9
The dolphins come

No amount of reasoning, discussion or persuasion by her father could make Alison change her mind the next morning. Their argument was brought to an end by the doorbell. Alison opened the front door to find Gareth standing there.

"It's too windy and cold for swimming today," he said, "but I thought you might like to go for a walk on the beach."

Her first impulse was to refuse. Then she changed her mind. Gareth looked tired and lonely. The death of his grandmother had upset him too. Besides, she would have to tell him that she was returning to Canada. For the first time she felt a small pang of regret. She would miss Gareth. That was the only thing she would miss about this horrible place, she added to herself resentfully.

They walked down to the beach in silence, the cat following along unobtrusively, as usual. Finally, as they stood together looking out over the waves, Gareth turned to Alison. "Did your father tell you Meiriona might be going with you to Canada this autumn?" he asked.

"Yes." The tone of Alison's voice left no doubt as to how she felt about it.

"Do you mind so much?"

"Yes."

"But Alison, don't you want to see your father happy?"

"I don't see why he needs Meiriona to be happy," she burst out. "We were perfectly happy before. And anyway," she added, "don't you mind that she's deserting you?"

"I don't think she's deserting me. I'm delighted that she'll have a more interesting life. And I'll be visiting on holidays — I might even stay there too. And I'll bring my cat! Just think of it, Alison. It means we'll be able to go on seeing each other. Doesn't that please you?" He paused for a moment, then added shyly, "It does me, you know."

Alison stared down at the sand and scuffed at a pebble with her toe. "Of course," she said. "But — "

"Let's forget that right now, though," Gareth went on, changing the subject abruptly. "There's something I've been wanting to ask you ever since I came back from Aberystwyth, but I've not had the chance. Before I left you said you wanted to ask me something — to talk about the house. Has anything happened to you there? Anything strange?"

Alison kept her eyes on the sand. "It — it wasn't really important," she said. "Anyway, it doesn't matter now. Now that I'm going back home."

"Going back! You're going back to Canada now?"

She bit her lip. This wasn't the way she had planned to tell him. "Yes," she said.

"But why?" He stared at her. "Is it because of Meiriona? It *is*, isn't it? You mind that much?"

Alison blushed. "It's not that I don't like Meiriona," she protested. "It's just that I don't want her to be with us. You don't understand. We've had such fun together, Dad and I. A stranger coming in — she'll just spoil it! You don't understand!" she repeated desperately.

"I do, Alison," Gareth said. "I really do. I can see how close you are to your father, and I can understand why you don't want anything or anyone to change that. But you're making a big mistake. Changes do happen, and there's not a thing you or I can do about it."

They fell silent. The wind had almost died down for the moment, but the waves were still whipping onto the beach. There was a tingly, almost electric feeling to the air. Alison finally raised her eyes to look at Gareth. He was watching her with an uneasy, intent look — almost as he had on the evening of their picnic.

"That's not all that's bothering you, though, is it?" he asked.

Suddenly, whether she was leaving or not, Alison had to confide in him. "No, it's not," she burst out. "Gareth, is Pen-y-Craig haunted?" As soon as the words were out of her mouth she felt like a fool. "Never mind. Forget —"

"Yes," Gareth answered.

It took a second for his answer to sink in.

"It is? You mean — you know?"

"I don't know. But my grandmam — remember what she said to you?"

"How could I forget it?"

"She — she always felt there was an evil aura around the house. She hated it. She said old Mrs. Evans hated it too. So much that for her last few years she moved out and lived in a small cottage in the village."

"So that's what your grandmother meant, then, when she said she couldn't bear it either," Alison murmured. "We never knew that. We thought she lived there until she died."

"No, I should think you wouldn't know that. The estate people wouldn't be repeating ghost stories to you when they handed over the house, would they? Besides, even if they did know about it, they'd just think it was all a pack of nonsense."

"But what happened?" she asked.

"I don't know. I don't even think my grandmam knew. But it *is* an unhappy house — I've felt it myself. Do you want to tell me what's happened to you?"

"Yes." With a rush of pure relief Alison poured out the whole story, beginning with the vision that had led her to the diary and ending with Bronwen's plea for help. When she finished, she turned away from Gareth and looked back up the beach towards the point. The relief was already fading, the fear and confusion returning. Would he believe her?

"What are you going to do?" he asked. There was no doubt of her in his voice. He had accepted her story, just as she'd told it, with no questions.

"I'm going home."

"You're not going to help her?"

"Help her? Help a *ghost*? How could I possibly do that?"

Gareth just shook his head.

"Gareth, be sensible! It's none of my business. I don't want to get involved. Besides," she added weakly, "I'm afraid."

"I know," he said. He raised his head and looked past her, almost as if he were listening to something. Something she had no way of hearing. He was about to say more when a movement far out to sea caught his attention.

"Look!" he cried. "Look there!"

Alison shaded her eyes with her hand and stared out to where he was pointing. She saw a dark, torpedo-like shape emerge from the water, twist gracefully, then fall back. Close behind it surfaced another, then another and another. "What are they?" she cried.

"Dolphins," he answered, his voice hushed.

Alison and Gareth stood side by side in silence as they watched the creatures playing and leaping in and out of the surf. In contrast to the darting, slightly comical seals, they looked sleek and powerful. Awe-inspiring.

"They say you see dolphins here only when there's a terrible storm coming." Gareth said. "I've never seen them this far south myself. It's very rare. Some say they only come when something really unusual is going to happen."

Alison looked up at the sky. The tense, electric feeling in the air was stronger than ever, and huge black clouds hovered over the horizon. The air was unusually clear. There seemed to be a waiting stillness hanging all around them.

Something wasn't right about the beach, though, she thought. Something was missing. Then she realized the screaming seabirds that always swooped and dove over their heads were nowhere to be seen. The absence of their constant cries added an even more eerie, uncanny feeling to the beach.

"The seagulls," she said. "They're gone."

"They know when a storm's coming too," Gareth answered. "They always go in." He had his head raised again in that same listening attitude. He almost seemed to be sniffing the air, and there was a look of profound uneasiness about him.

"I'd better get back," Alison said apprehensively. She was suddenly cold and shivering.

The dolphins had disappeared. They watched for them for a moment, then with one accord they turned and walked back towards the cliff path.

"Alison," Gareth said slowly. "If anything happens tonight — if you get into any kind of trouble — will you call me?" He turned to look down at her and his eyes looked dark almost to the point of blackness.

"What can happen?" she answered, trying to sound offhand. But her voice was shaky. "I'm going back to Pen-y-Craig, and most likely by tomorrow I'll be on my way to Canada. I'll be glad to see you again when you come to visit, but I want to get as far away from here as possible and forget everything about it."

"It might not be that easy," Gareth said. But he wasn't looking at her any longer, and it sounded almost as if he were speaking to himself rather than to her. Then he turned back to her. "Remember," he said with an intensity that was almost fierce, "call me."

"Of course," Alison answered. "But nothing's going to happen. I'll see you tomorrow and let you know when I'm leaving. So we can say goodbye." She faltered over the last words, then turned and ran towards the looming old house, Gareth's voice echoing in her mind: "Call me." He must have spoken without thinking, as she had answered "of course" without thinking. How could she possibly call him? They had no telephone.

At the front door she almost ran into Meiriona, who was just coming out. Her face was curiously flushed. "Oh, I'm sorry!" Alison stammered. She stepped aside and made as if to go on past her.

"Alison, wait." Meiriona caught her arm.

Alison stopped and looked at her.

"I've just been speaking with your father," Meiriona said. Her words sounded stilted and unnatural, not like her usual happy, lilting voice at all. "He's told me how upset you are about the idea of my going to Canada. He says you're going back home now because of me. Is that true?"

Alison could feel her cheeks beginning to burn. At the same time, all the resentment and dislike she felt for Meiriona surfaced uncontrollably. "Yes, I am," she answered defiantly. "I won't be around to bother you anymore."

"You don't bother me, Alison. I like you. I was worried about you when you got hurt. I was hoping we could be good friends. I never had a sister . . ."

Alison pressed her lips together as tightly as she could to stop their trembling. She felt as if she were on fire inside. Meiriona seemed to be waiting for her to say something, but finally she gave up. The colour had risen in her cheeks too. Almost unconsciously, it seemed, she squared her shoulders as she met Alison's stare head on.

"I've never caused unhappiness or strife in anyone's family," Meiriona said, "and I'll not be the cause of trouble between you and your father." She was struggling to keep her voice level. "I was perfectly satisfied with my life here before you came, and I'm sure I'll be just as satisfied after you leave."

In spite of herself there was a slight tremor in her voice, and she shook her head angrily before she went on. "I'm not going to Canada. I'll finish out my studies here." She dropped Alison's arm and, before Alison could collect herself, turned and walked — almost ran — down the path away from her.

Alison continued on into the house, her mind

in a turmoil. She should have felt happy, triumphant — she had won. But she didn't. More than ever she just wanted to leave! To escape and leave this confusion behind her.

She headed immediately for her room, but her father appeared out of the seldom-used living room and blocked the hall. His face was thunderous. "She won't come," he said. "Because of you. She won't come! Are you satisfied now?"

Choking back a sob, Alison pushed past him and ran up the stairs. Unconsciously she ran into Bronwen's room instead of her own. Once inside, realizing what she'd done, she half turned to run out again, then stood still. She looked around her. The room was quiet. And empty.

"I'm leaving." Defiantly Alison spoke the words into the silence. "I'm leaving, Bronwen. I can't help you."

Then, unable to stop herself, she looked towards the fireplace. One last time. There probably wasn't anything legible left in the diary anyway, but she'd look at it one last time. Strangely enough, she wasn't frightened anymore. Meiriona's words, her father's stricken face, were too fresh in her memory. She jerked the book open roughly and leafed through the pages savagely, as if the diary were to blame for everything that had happened. Suddenly a page leaped out at her in ink so dark and clear it looked as if it had been written that very day. *I saw the dolphins today!* it began, jolting her to attention. She stared at the writing, hardly able to believe what she was reading.

*They say that means a storm is coming. Father told
me the last time the dolphins were seen around here
there was a terrible wreck. A ship had come into our
harbour for shelter from the storm and then the
wind shifted suddenly and drove her onto the rocks.
She foundered right before the eyes of everyone on
shore, and every man aboard her was drowned. I'm
sure there will be a storm tonight too, as all the
birds have gone in and it's deathly quiet. The sea
has been unusually rough all day, and the waters
look grey and dismal — all full of clay and sand.*

*I was so intrigued with the dolphins that I did
a very stupid thing. Father would be furious if he
ever found out. I was watching them from a rock at
the mouth of Noddwr and I didn't realize the tide
had reached the point and cut me off! I've never
been so frightened in my life. I started to run for the
point, but realized it was useless and came back to
the cave. Then I remembered all the stories about
the cave being an old smugglers' hideout, and I
began to think that if this were so they must have
had some way of getting up and down to it by the
cliffs. I searched and searched. There are only
patches of brown and green grass on the rocks there,
and bracken and low bushes. No place to hide a
path, one would think. It took me a long time to find
it, and just in time. I am still shivering at the
memory of it. The water was lapping at my feet
when I found the first toehold! Once I was started I
could follow it up easily enough, although it's very
steep, but no one would ever imagine it was there by*

just looking at the cliff from either the top or the bottom.

It rather pleases me that I have found this secret way to and from my cave. I shan't tell anyone about it, least of all Catrin. She would be certain to tell father, and he would forbid me to use it. And she would say that he was right, of course. She always takes his side against me and pretends to think he's so wonderful. She thinks I can't see through her, but I can. She's ——

The writing stopped here abruptly with a long slash of ink, as if Bronwen had been suddenly interrupted. Alison turned the page quickly and the words went on, dark and angry, written with such furious force that they almost seemed to be etched into the page.

She's won! Catrin has won. Just as I was writing the last page she knocked at the door and came in, hardly giving me time to hide my diary under my skirt. She was smiling such a victorious smile I knew at once something dreadful had happened, as it has.

She is to marry my father! She told me such a deal of nonsense about loving him and loving me, but I don't believe a word of it. Does she really think she can take my mother's place? She has won and there will be no room for me in this house now. There is no room for me anywhere. My father was the only one I had left, and he has deserted me. She

*said that my father was waiting outside to speak to
me himself about it, but that they thought it would
be better if she told me first. I refused to see him. I
won't speak to him and I shan't speak to her again
either.*

The writing grew more and more shaky and
uncontrolled. Large blots, as of tears, smeared
many of the words and Alison could hardly make
them out. There were several words that she
couldn't read at all, then:

*I'll go to my cave tonight after they're all asleep.
I'll stay there until the waters come for me, and that
will put an end to it. There's nothing else to do.*

The diary ended there.

Is that what happened? Alison wondered,
searching frantically through the rest of the blank
pages. Did Bronwen drown herself? Somehow she
just couldn't accept that. There had to be something else.

She looked around her into the shadows that
were growing thick in the darkening room. Suddenly she knew Bronwen was there. Still, she
wasn't afraid. A sense of despair and anguish
seemed to be filling the room, surrounding her. In
desperation she turned back to the last entry in the
diary and read it again.

Then she turned the page, and there was one
small paragraph more. In her first feverish hurry
to see what else had been written, she had turned

two pages at once and had missed it. The writing was wild — so blotched and blotted with tears it was impossible to read. Alison stared at it, willing the words to make themselves clear to her.

She followed me! Somehow she must have known where I would be and she followed me down to Noddwr! At the very last moment, just as the waters were coming up to the cave — cold and dark, oh, so terribly cold and dark — I grew more frightened than I could bear and dashed for the secret path I found this afternoon. I started to climb and when I was halfway up I heard Catrin call me from the cave! She must have gone in just after I ran out. I knew she was trapped. I knew the tide had cut her off, and I heard her call me — but I didn't go back. Oh, dear God, I didn't go back!

With these words the diary really did end. Alison sat unable to move. Tears poured down her cheeks, but she made no motion to wipe them away. Finally she knew what the tragedy of Pen-y-Craig had been. Poor Catrin. Poor Bronwen. How had she gone on living, knowing she had caused another human being to be drowned? What must the rest of her life have been like?

Far away over the ocean Alison heard the rumble and roll of thunder, and the wind, which had died down, sprang up again and snatched at the curtains.

But I still don't know what I can do, Alison thought hopelessly. She looked again at that last, desperate paragraph, then turned back to the beginning of the entry.

I saw the dolphins today! she read again. Just as *she* had seen them. She glanced at the date, and suddenly she knew.

The twenty-second of July, she breathed. That's today! And today I saw the dolphins too!

Alison stood up, put the little book back carefully and went over to the window. The sea was rough and grey, just as Bronwen had described it, and the clouds were gathering for the storm.

"Tonight is her second chance," Alison whispered aloud. "That must be it. And if I'm there . . . maybe I can change it . . . maybe I can stop her. That must be what I'm meant to do."

10
An end and a beginning

Alison's father didn't call her down to supper that evening. She stayed in her room until well after dark, listening to the silence. His typewriter was not tapping; he wasn't working. The storm was still rumbling and threatening in the distance. The air seemed incredibly still and charged with electricity.

Alison walked restlessly around her room. Finally she heard her father's steps on the stairs and the slam of the door as he went into his room. His footsteps had sounded slow and tired, and for a moment she felt guilty. Then she knelt down and quickly pulled her tennis shoes on — they were soft-soled and would be better than her sandals for climbing the cliff in the dark if she had to. Quietly she slipped out of her room, closing the door carefully behind her. She crept down the stairs.

She opened the back door and took the latch off, shutting it tightly behind her. The wind was getting stronger and she didn't want the door banging. The moon was shining as she left the house, but just as she started across the garden a cloud crossed in front of it and the cliffs were plunged into darkness. Alison looked up. She could see no stars at all. The sky was thick with clouds and she knew that the moon wouldn't be coming back out.

As she watched, lightning flashed far out over the sea, and the slow rumble of thunder reached her. She stared at the pitch-black garden in front of her and was suddenly filled with such an intense dread that it was all she could do not to pull open the door behind her and rush back into the house. "Go on," she whispered to herself. "You have to!"

Cautiously she crossed the garden and opened the little gate in the wall. It shrieked on its rusty hinges as she pulled it, and she caught her breath in alarm. She froze, listening. Nothing. The wind was blowing harder now, and the surf pounding at the rocks below the cliff must have covered the noise. She slipped through the gate, her heart thumping heavily and her fingers trembling as she propped it open for her return. Then she ran towards the path to the beach.

When Alison reached the beach she looked out towards the ocean and drew in a sharp breath of dismay. The tide was almost in. Was she too late? Recklessly she ran over the pebbly beach towards the point, stumbling and tripping in the dark. As she reached it, the first fat, heavy drops of rain started to fall, slapping against her cheeks with amazing force. The tide was almost up to the rocks of the point and she raced to get around it in time. She must get to the cave and help Bronwen!

But when she reached the cave it took only a moment to realize that it was empty. It *was* too late. Then for a brief moment lightning flashed, just long enough for her to see footprints in the damp sand — two sets coming into the cave, hers and one other, and one set going back out and on down to the beach. She started to follow them. The waves were almost up to her now, cold and dark, just as Bronwen had seen them. She stared at them, hypnotized with terror and unable to move. They flashed white in the blackness, and when lightning lit up the dark mass of water behind them, it seemed to reach for her like a hungry monster. Just then, from the point, a voice cried out, startling her back to her senses.

Bronwen!

The spell was broken. It was Catrin. Another flash of lightning lit up the sand, showing her the direction of Bronwen's footsteps, towards the secret path up the cliff. She began to run along after them. Suddenly they turned in towards the cliff face and stopped. Alison stretched out her arms to the sheer rock in front of her, feeling desperately for the crevice she knew must be there. Her nails broke and tore as she scraped them across the stubbly rock. Then she found it. Almost of its own accord her foot found the first toehold and, miraculously, the path opened up above her. She climbed desperately, almost running in places where the path widened and flattened out enough for her to stand upright.

A shower of stones fell down on her from

above. Looking up, she saw a dark shape above her. At the same time a voice called out again from below.

Bronwen!

The shape stopped and looked down. Alison looked down too and saw the first ripples of water reaching greedily towards the cliff.

Bronwen!

There was now a note of panic in the voice calling from below. Bronwen looked down for another long moment, then turned and started to climb again.

Alison shrieked after her. "Stop! You *must* stop!"

Once more Bronwen hesitated, but this time Alison kept on climbing. She had to reach her! Bronwen *had* to go back!

At a place where the path widened, just below Bronwen, Alison cried out again to the dark figure above her. "It's Catrin calling, Bronwen. You've got to go back and get her!"

She was screaming by now and weeping, the tears streaming down her cheeks and mingling with the rain that was slashing at them. The wind had increased in fury. Alison had to hang onto the rocks with all her strength to keep from being blown off the path.

Bronwen stopped. The voice from below was calling more desperately than ever.

"Go back, Bronwen," Alison sobbed. "Go back!"

Bronwen pressed her face close to the rock.

Alison saw her sway and almost fall. Instinctively she reached up to steady her, but just then Bronwen turned her head and looked down at the sea crashing below. A sudden flash of lightning seemed to linger. In the unnatural light Bronwen straightened, paused, then started to climb back down. When she reached the ledge where Alison was clinging, Alison started to speak to her. But Bronwen stared through her as if she couldn't see her and kept on going down.

Alison peered after her into the blackness, but she couldn't see anything. Finally two figures emerged out of the void, climbing up towards her. She shrank back against the rock, but they took no notice of her. Bronwen was helping a young woman. Alison caught only a glimpse of a pale, terrified face as they passed her and climbed on up. Dodging a small shower of stones, she watched them until they disappeared out of sight over the top of the cliff. Then she sank back down onto the path.

At that moment the fall of stones that Bronwen and Catrin had dislodged became more ominous. Larger stones began to fall, then rocks. Alison looked up. To her horror, she saw the whole top of the cliff dissolving into a river of mud and rocks pouring down towards her.

"Gareth!" she screamed uselessly, unreasonably, as the viscous, sliding mass engulfed her. "Gareth!"

The landslide beat down on her for what seemed like an eternity. Desperately she held onto the cliff, but one by one her fingers began losing their grip. Suddenly she lost hold completely. She was falling, swept along by the mud. After a long, panic-stricken moment, she felt herself land on a ledge with a thud. She grabbed onto a bush, and burying her face in her arms, huddled in a ball as the last of the slide poured over her.

Stones hit her head, her shoulders, her arms. When they finally stopped she lay exhausted, unable to move. She lost all sense of time. She had no idea how long she had lain there when she heard someone call her name.

"Alison!"

Incredibly, it was Gareth. He was working his way carefully down the mud and rocks from the top of the cliff.

"How did you know — " Alison began.

"There's no time. I'll explain later." His voice was urgent. "It's still pouring rain and there's liable to be another slide at any moment. We've got to get out of here. Do you think you can climb if I help you?"

Alison sat up cautiously, not letting go of her lifesaving bush. Instinctively she looked down, but was glad she couldn't see below her in the howling darkness. The waves sounded wild and angry as they crashed onto the rocks at the foot of the cliff. When she moved, every part of her felt bruised. "I can climb," she said, gritting her teeth.

As a flash of lightning lit up Gareth's face, she saw he was grinning at her. Suddenly, in spite of everything, Alison felt lighter and happier than she had since they'd walked into Pen-y-Craig. She let go of the bush to take his hand.

Slowly, bit by bit, they worked their way up. At the top they fell down onto the soaking grass at the cliff's edge and lay panting. Lightning flashed almost continuously now, lighting up the garden of Pen-y-Craig. Alison looked towards the house itself. It was dark and mysterious in the shadows, but somehow it no longer seemed sinister. Even though the rain and the cold were making her shiver violently, a strange feeling of peace flooded through her. She looked towards Bronwen's room, but the window was closed and empty. Alison knew she would never see Bronwen again.

Gareth followed her gaze. "Bronwen?" he asked.

"She's all right now," Alison answered. "Tomorrow — I'll tell you what happened tomorrow." Then she looked at him. "How did you know I needed you?" she asked. "How did you know where to find me?"

"You called me," Gareth answered. "I heard."

"But you couldn't have," she objected.

"I did, though."

It was impossible. But no more impossible than anything else that had happened. Alison clung to Gareth's hand.

"You'd better get in now," he said gently. "I'll come over tomorrow." He hesitated for a moment, suddenly unsure. "Will — will you still be going back to Canada?"

"No," she answered. "I think I can stay here now. And Gareth —" She stopped.

"Yes?"

"Will you tell Meiriona I'm sorry. Tell her — I

was wrong." She looked back towards the cliff and shuddered to think of the cave below now filled with swirling black water. "As wrong as Bronwen was about Catrin," she added in a whisper that couldn't be heard above the wind.

As she let herself into the house she noticed that the wind seemed to be dying down at last. Lightning was flashing less and less. Thunder muttered grouchily in the distance for a moment longer, then died away altogether. Inside the kitchen a few coals still glowed in the fireplace, shedding small flickers of light. It felt warm, safe and secure.

Alison didn't sleep well the rest of that night. She was up with the first weak light of dawn. The storm was over, although it was still cloudy and dull. She got out of bed and pulled on a long-sleeved shirt to cover the bruises on her arms. Aching all over from the pummelling she had taken the night before, she went down the hall to Bronwen's room. Once inside, she closed the door behind her and crossed over to the fireplace as she had done so many times before. But today there was a difference. For the first time, the room felt like any other ordinary room.

Alison pulled out the diary, but before she opened it, she walked over to the window and pulled it wide, letting in a rush of damp, sea-smelling air. Standing there, she leafed through the fragile book carefully until she came to the last entry: *I saw the dolphins today!*

Once again she read Bronwen's final, sad

sentence: *I'll go to my cave tonight after they're all asleep. I'll stay there until the waters come for me, and that will put an end to it. There's nothing else to do.*

Then, with trembling hands, Alison turned the page. This was what she had come for. Instead of the blotched, tear-stained paragraph she remembered, there was a full page of neat, almost joyous writing. Hardly daring to breathe, she began to read:

The most wonderful thing has happened! I went to Noddwr tonight, but when the dark, cold waters started to come towards me I suddenly became terribly frightened and dashed for my secret path. Then, as I was climbing, I heard Catrin calling from below — she had followed me! I stopped, but decided to go on anyway. Catrin was no concern of mine, and if she was silly enough to follow me it wasn't my fault, was it? But the strangest thing happened. I seemed to hear a voice telling me to stop. Over and over it begged me to go back, and I realized that Catrin would surely drown if I didn't. I could not let that happen. I climbed back down and the water was already lapping at the rocks. Catrin was standing at the mouth of the cave, not even noticing the tide swirling around her ankles, calling my name.

When she saw me she burst into tears and came running towards me. She hugged me and kissed me, crying out, "You're safe, Bronwen. Oh, thank God you're safe!" She wasn't even aware of her own danger. I was so surprised I couldn't say a word. Then, when I recovered myself, I realized that we both had to hurry or we would be trapped. I shouted to her to follow me and somehow or other I managed to get her up the path. She is not a very good climber.

When we reached the top we collapsed into each other's arms — I don't know which of us was weeping the harder. And then she said the most extraordinary thing. She actually offered to go away! She said she hadn't realized the thought of her marrying my father would make me so unhappy that I would try to drown myself. She said she loved me far too much to cause me any more suffering. And this time I believed her. She vowed that even though she loved my father as much as life itself, she would give him up and go far away just for me.

I have been so selfish and blind. I've been unhappy and jealous and I've misjudged Catrin completely. I can see now that I didn't even try to believe her. I begged her to stay, to live with father and me from now on, and she has promised she will. Somehow I feel that an old, unhappy chapter of my life is over now, and stretching out ahead of me is a bright new beginning.

And yet, I have a strange feeling. A very strange feeling that perhaps I've been more fortunate than I realize — almost as if I've been given a second chance. And this time I must make no mistakes. I think I shall put this book away now and not write in it again. It will lie buried behind the bricks forever, and with it will lie buried all that old hate and unhappiness. A new beginning deserves a new diary, and this one may rest in peace.

Alison closed the book and put it away in its niche for the last time. Now the diary could "rest in peace" indeed. She looked up and around at the room. The sun had come out at last and was pouring in, while a slight breeze ruffled the curtains gently. The air coming in from the sea smelled clean and new-washed. Outside, the seagulls and kittiwakes wheeled and cried and dove down to the wavetops once more in their ceaseless search for fish. Bronwen was gone. Alison could feel it. She had had her new beginning after all.

"And I'll have my new beginning as well," Alison whispered. It would be fun having Meiriona around. What was it she had said? She had never had a sister. Neither had Alison. It would certainly be different!

And Gareth. She smiled happily to herself at the thought of him. Maybe they would never understand what had happened last night, maybe they would never be able to explain it, but there was no way she wanted to leave him now. She had begun to understand just a little bit how her father felt about Meiriona.

Alison stood up and walked out of the room, closing the door carefully behind her. She looked towards her father's door. She had a lot of making up to do there. A good solid breakfast of pancakes and bacon would do for a start, she decided blithely. She headed down the stairs towards the kitchen, humming.

Karleen Bradford was born in Ontario and lived in Canada until she was nine years old. She moved with her parents to Argentina, but returned to Canada to attend university. Later she married a Foreign Service Officer, and they and their three children have lived in Columbia and Brazil, the United States, England and the Philippines. Karleen has produced four earlier books and several short stories, and has won several grants and prizes for her writing. She is currently working on several new projects, as well as touring and lecturing. She has also acquired pilot and scuba-diving licences in her "spare" time!